OUTER VOICES
INNER LIVES

A Collection of LGBTQ
Writers Over 50

CONTENTS

"Life is like the river, sometimes it sweeps you gently along and sometimes the rapids come out of nowhere."

– Emma Smith

FOREWORD

Through the ages, any culture that hoped to endure was compelled to cherish and protect its treasury of older people, with all their accumulated memories, experience and information. Today we LGBT people pride ourselves on our arrival as a culture. But we are just now learning to cherish our own elders—not just the iconic figures with international visibility, but also the rank-and-file citizens whose seasoned views might have a more local influence.

Yet our elders face more challenges than just the bias in favor of "youth and beauty" held by many in the LGBT world. As a result of economic turmoil and sparse civil-rights protection for LGBT people, the threats to our seniors' jobs, housing, credit and healthcare are intensified by the fact of their age. Not to mention the growing threat of U. S. senior homelessness, which is expected to double by 2050. Often LGBT elders who have enjoyed long-term relationships, whether legally married or not, find that many retirement homes and assisted-living facilities refuse to deal with same-sex couples.

Beyond these horizons of crisis, it's vital for LGBT literature to record that differing angle from which life is viewed by the older lesbian, gay man, bisexual and transgendered or intersex person. Those who lived through World War II or the Stonewall Rebellion often have a take on today's events that varies from the take of young Millennials.

Last but not least, cultures have found comfort in simply hearing from their older living persons who have been through it all – spiritual grandparents who can help a younger generation sort things out.

Hence the timeliness and value of this anthology, which brings together a treasure of 16 powerful short stories by authors over 50.

– Patricia Nell Warren

INTRODUCTION

We feel invisible. It's an oft-heard and common experience for people once they pass a sort of age-demarcation line in our society, and in our own LGBTQ communities. It was among the reasons we started lgbtSr.org and RainbowGray.com, websites where our lives could be expressed as going concerns, showing those of us over 50 in our vibrancy, creativity and collective knowledge. We wanted to provide spaces where we are very visible, where we see our lives reflected and share the richness of our experiences and personal journeys. And while we launched these unaware of each other, we have since become friends, with a shared mission to our audience, and now co-editors for this collection.

Outer Voices Inner Lives is a natural progression of that desire to air our voices, to let ourselves be heard. In this collection you'll meet rich and poor, widowed and partnered, young, older and old. Gay, lesbian, bisexual, trans. Ultimately human: that's what we are once the definitions are put away. Human beings living an arc, with every moment of that arc, every stage of life, as vital and immediate as the others. *Age is not something we are, it's something we do.* Like trees and elephants and rivers. The river's end flows as mightily as its beginning.

You'll find 16 distinct stories here, 16 authors whose imaginations spark and ignite. In the light of those sparks you'll find the lives of people who are not invisible, not disappeared, not silent, whether they're 40, 60 or 80.

Here's to never being silent, to remaining in our light on that stage until its very last flickering. There is no room we need to make for anyone, no premature exit for the next, younger, occupant, because the room is our own.

- Mark McNease & Stephen Dolainski

MANATEE GARDENS

Jean Ryan

They were sitting in the too-warm kitchen, drinking instant coffee. Peggy looked past her mother's head and through the window. Snow was falling in the backyard, covering tree limbs, mounding in the stone bird bath. At the top of the window hung a plastic Santa with a sack slung over his shoulder and the words Merry Christmas beneath his boots. This was a reliable decoration, appearing each year at this time, and much of the paint had flecked off. Peggy turned her gaze back to the lazy Susan and with one finger slowly spun it round. She had done this as a child, watched these same items revolve: a jar of instant coffee, a white sugar bowl, a pair of ribbed salt and pepper shakers. From the rug beside the back door, Frankie, the aging fox terrier Jan had rescued from the pound, yawned audibly.

"What do you want for Christmas?" Peggy asked.

"I want to swim with the manatees," Jan said.

Peggy stopped the lazy Susan and gaped at her mother. "Since when?"

"I love manatees," Jan said fiercely. Her blue eyes flashed. As if in defiance of her seventy-eight years, her eyes were bright and still beautiful. As always, her hair was pulled off her face and tied in a ponytail; she had been a natural blonde and the transition to silver had been subtle.

Peggy frowned. It was just like her mother to say this sort of thing, to come up with some sudden, peculiar whim, probably fueled by a program she'd seen.

"You get on a boat and go to them," Jan went on. "You wear a wetsuit."

"Where's this?'

"Florida. I have a brochure." Jan rose stiffly and opened a drawer behind her. As usual, she was wearing black stirrup pants and one of the aggressively cheerful sweatshirts she bought at the mall. Peggy noted how small her mother's back looked now, how thin her calves had become. It was true: she was shrinking.

"Manatee Gardens, it's called." She pulled a flyer out of the drawer and slid it across the table. Peggy glanced at the photos: a catamaran, a grinning captain, turquoise water studded with fat brown humps.

"They're closed on Christmas day but not on Christmas eve," Jan said. "That's when I want to go."

Peggy looked up from the brochure. "Are you kidding? It'll be a zoo!"

Jan shook her head. "It's not a zoo. It's their home."

Merging onto the Pike, Peggy thought, *why manatees?* If her mother wanted to swim with dolphins or turtles, like everybody else, they'd be headed to the Bahamas or Maui, not some Florida tourist trap. She could see the place now: a worn-out gift shop with key chain bobbles and dusty jiggers, a few torpid reptiles in smudged terrariums, a leather-skinned, bleary-eyed skipper handing out life vests to shrieking children.

At least her mother had given up the notion of holiday travel and agreed to a mid-January trip. And it wasn't like they'd be gone very long—a three-day weekend would probably suffice. And even if they weren't heading for some swank Caribbean resort, at least they'd be getting a respite from the brown snowbanks and ice-crusted sidewalks of the eastern Massachusetts. They would make the most of this trip, Peggy decided, changing lanes, and her lips tightened in accordance.

She would take care of the travel plans, she told her mother, and Jan had shrugged. "Okay," she said. "But no frills." What Peggy really wanted to do was get a peek at her mother's checkbook. Not long ago, Jan had written a generous check to a crook who appeared at her door asking for donations for children in need of facial surgery. "He was wearing a suit," she explained.

It wasn't just her mother's trusting nature that concerned Peggy; it was her recent difficulty with words. Today she'd been fine, but when they met for lunch a month ago, Jan had opened her mouth to order a sandwich and had not been able to speak. "I want," she began, and then her eyes widened and she looked at Peggy for help. Peggy blinked at her. "What do you want, Mom?" Jan said nothing, just shook her head. Peggy reached across the table and laid a hand on her mother's arm. "Just point to it," she said, and Jan did as she was told, tapped the picture of the grilled cheese sandwich and nodded at the waiter. Peggy ordered her own sandwich, and when the waiter left she turned back to her mother. She was going to tell her it was fine, that everyone forgets their words now and then, when Jan smiled at her and said, "Well wasn't that the damndest thing."

"The brain is circuitry," her husband explained that night. Philip was a vascular surgeon at Brigham Hospital. "With age, disease, the wiring fails." Peggy pictured this, wires sparking and shorting, parts going dark. And her mother was aware of this, knew that her mind had turned treacherous. Peggy could not think of anything more dreadful, and she was baffled by her mother's calm—at least she *seemed* calm.

A check-up and cognitive tests revealed nothing, nothing tragic at any rate—manageable degrees of osteoporosis and arthritis, slightly elevated blood pressure; all her labs were normal. As for Jan's language difficulties, there were drugs they could try if the condition worsened. "But we'll sit tight for now," the doctor said, rising from his chair. Jan turned to Peggy. "I told you I was fine. Now let's get out of here."

⚬⚬⚬

Snow and heavy traffic hampered the trip home, and it took Peggy nearly an hour to drive from Shrewsbury to Newton, a commute she made every couple weeks. One day her mother would probably be living with them, which would solve the travel concerns, but Peggy could not yet allow herself to contemplate this arrangement; each time the thought crept up, she pushed it back down. Philip was actually fine with the notion of Jan moving in, maybe because he had lost his own parents many years before, or maybe because he simply and truly liked Jan. He said she was "a kick." Jan *was* a kick, Peggy agreed, but this had no bearing on what her daily presence here would do. Peggy loved her husband for his generosity, but really, he had no idea.

She walked into her house and switched on the hall sconces. At some point in the afternoon, witnessed by no one, the roses on the granite table had fallen from their stems, and the white petals on the black surface looked like art. She stood there a moment, admiring this small gift, before hanging up her coat and heading into the sleek kitchen with its cherry cabinets and stainless steel appliances. This was an older Craftsman home, but renovations over the past five years had turned each room new and close to flawless.

Philip had surgeries today and would not be home till at least 7:00. Peggy poured herself a glass of Pinot Gris and fixed a small plate of goat cheese and crackers, which she carried into the study and set beside the computer. She needed to make flight reservations

4

right away and to see what sort of accommodations she could secure at this late date. Jan did not want Peggy paying for this trip, but Peggy was firm, reminding her that this was a Christmas present, and it was. It was also insurance. They didn't have to stay at the Grand Hyatt, but Peggy would not have them wind up in one of those budget monstrosities, besieged each spring by crazed college students.

⇥ ⇤

For the flight to Tampa, Jan brought a box of art markers and a book of circular designs, which she steadily filled in with color. Peggy, who had never seen a coloring book intended for adults, asked her mother where she found it.

"Amazon," said Jan. "It's called 'active meditation.'" She slid a teal marker out of the pack. "These are mandalas—sacred circles. They're supposed to be calming."

Peggy smiled. "Are you calm yet?"

Jan shrugged. "I just like coloring them in. It's something to do." She looked up at Peggy. "You want one?"

"No thanks. I have my book." But the writing was god-awful—Dan Brown should have stopped after *The Da Vinci Code*. She kept looking up from the page and out the window, where crumpled mountain ranges and patchwork farmland slowly slid beneath them; to the left was the shimmering Atlantic. She checked her watch: one more hour.

"I think I'll take one of those pictures, Mom."

Jan set down her marker and carefully pulled a page—they were perforated— from the back of the book. She handed it Peggy, then bent back over her work. "Start on the outside," she advised. Peggy pulled an orange marker out of the pack and began coloring in the border of an intricate circle. "My god," she breathed. "I see angels." Her mother ignored this, and after a few minutes, Peggy found herself absorbed in her picture, giving thought to the shades she chose and leaning back to see the effect. When she heard the pilot announcing their descent, she was surprised.

Jan pushed up her tray table and tucked the mandala book back in her bag. She looked about the plane with pleasant interest, then leaned back and closed her eyes. Peggy regarded her profile wistfully, thinking how pretty her mother was, how good her neck and chin still looked. Peggy would not be that lucky, did not have that sort of bone structure. She was fifty-five and doubted anyone would guess her any younger. From her father she had inherited her square jaw, as well as her tallness, and now that her estrogen was gone, she had his waistline, too.

"Is Carolyn taking care of Frankie?" Peggy asked. Carolyn was Jan's next door neighbor and oldest friend. She too had lost her husband several years before.

Jan opened her eyes and turned to Peggy. "She's staying in the house, bless her heart."

"That's sweet of her. Frankie will like that."

Peggy looked out the window again. Tampa looked infinite. Toy cars moved along toy highways; here and there were the turquoise lozenges of swimming pools. The drive to Crystal River, she'd read, took about an hour and fifteen minutes; she'd have to remember to ask for a car with navigation.

"So mom," she said, turning back to Jan. "What is it about manatees? Why the big urge to see them?"

Her mother didn't speak for so long that Peggy thought she had once again lost the ability. Jan had never been a talker, which was frustrating at times, but better, Peggy supposed, than a mother who never shut up.

"You know they call them sea cows?" Jan said at last. "They're *huge*. They don't harm anything. They just swim around eating plants."

"Are you sure you'll get to see any?"

Jan nodded. "This place we're going, Kings Bay? The manatees go there every winter—they can't take cold water. It stops their digestion."

"I suppose they're endangered," said Peggy.

"Oh yes." Jan sighed. "Boats hit them."

Peggy waited for something more intriguing, but her mother had closed her eyes again and had nothing else to say.

It was late afternoon when they finally pulled into the hotel. Peggy's eyes were tired and she had a ferocious headache. Despite the car's navigation, they had taken the wrong exit twice and traffic had been terrible.

"I need a drink," Peggy said, stepping out of the car. "Pronto." Despite the thick cloud cover and cool temperature—66°F according to the rental car—she could feel the humidity close in around her. Across the parking lot, the hotel rose before them like a promise kept, just as attractive as its online photo.

"Sounds good," said Jan, who, with some effort, emerged from the car and looked around. She gestured at the hotel. "It's….."

Peggy waited a few seconds, then finished the sentence. "It's new. It's supposed to be nice. I'll check us in and be right back."

Their rooms were adjacent and located on the top floor, removed from footfalls and ice machine noise. Pushing open the reassuringly heavy door, Peggy paused to take in the amenities, gratified by the room's soothing colors, the immaculate king-size bed (wisely minus a spread), the faux mahogany furnishings. No matter how the rest of the weekend went, at least they had these separate, pleasing rooms in which to repair. Jan of course did not approve of this arrangement, had already protested the extravagance of two rooms. Peggy, knowing her mother would react this way, paid her no heed.

Frugality, Peggy had learned, was a habit, one she'd eventually broken free of. Thrift could get the better of you, could close a lot of doors. Her father had been frugal. For thirty-two years he owned a shoe store in downtown Shrewsbury, never changing out the old carousel racks or revamping the front windows, paying no attention to the more fashionable businesses that shouldered their way in. As a child, Peggy had loved her father's store, loved trying on all the new shoes and admiring them in the little floor mirrors, but as she got older these feelings changed, and the store became an embarrassment. For one thing, it was called Sheldon's Shoes, which would have been fine except that Sheldon was her father's first name. Sheldon's Shoes sounded like one of those elaborately illustrated children's books, a pair of penny loafers on the cover, all ready for their big day. The fact that nothing in the store changed, that year after year people sat on the same olive green Naugahyde seats and turned the same creaking displays depressed Peggy beyond speech, and when her father finally sold it, two years before he died, she was glad to lose the association. Predictably, her father's income had been modest, but if he had not been a canny businessman, he had been shrewd in other areas, surprising his bereaved widow with some well-timed investments and a life insurance policy that more than covered her monthly bills.

The desk clerk told them about a nice restaurant not far from the hotel, and so Peggy and Jan decided to walk there. A strong breeze blew against them as they made their way down the wide asphalt path that bordered the highway. How strange this place was, Peggy thought, this flat, open land with its random businesses stretched along the road, a pawn shop here, a hair salon there. Trees grew in disparate clumps, bare, twisting limbs entangled with ivy-choked pines. Lanky palm trees swayed in the wind, their fronds waving and snapping. Just as Peggy and Jan reached the restaurant, rain drops pattered their heads and shoulders.

"Hope it's not pouring when we leave," said Peggy, smoothing her hair. "Do they still give tours when it's raining?"

"I don't know why they wouldn't," Jan said.

The restaurant was dimly lit and nearly empty; it smelled of fried fish, varnished wood and a potent disinfectant. A smiling, chunky hostess led them to a booth and handed them large leather-bound menus. "Enjoy your evening," she said.

Peggy pulled her reading glasses out of her purse and opened the menu; Jan, who'd had refractive surgery, did not require glasses. "God almighty, look how small the print is—why do they *do* that?" She scanned the list, frowning. "Wow. They really nail the tourists here—$29 for a pork chop."

Jan closed her menu and said, "I'll have a Manhattan and the Vintage Seafood Platter."

Peggy set her menu on top of the other and removed her glasses. "Guess I'll have the grilled grouper."

A server appeared at their table, a black woman with thin glossy braids that fell over one shoulder. Tidy, perfect rows crisscrossed her scalp. "Can I get you ladies something from the bar?" she said. She had a Cajun drawl: half Deep South, half Caribbean.

"You sure can," said Peggy. "I'll have a Stoli over and she'll have a Manhattan."

"Be right back," said the woman, picking up the menus. Jan watched her walk away.

"I like her hair."

"Must take forever to do that," Peggy said.

"They call them cornrows," said Jan. "Black people spend a lot of money on their hair."

Peggy smiled. "How to you know that?"

"I saw a show. They buy hair and make 'weaves' out of it. Do you know where the hair comes from?"

Peggy shook her head.

"India. Indian women are afraid to go to sleep because people cut off their hair when they're sleeping." Jan nodded. "It's true."

Peggy, absorbing this, said, "Mom, you are one surprise after another."

Both their meals came with a salad: iceberg lettuce on ice cold plates with a few pallid wedges of tomatoes and some shredded carrot.

Peggy got through about half her salad, then watched Jan chase the last bits of carrot on her plate. For a small woman, her mother had an astonishing appetite.

"When do we have to be at Manatee Gardens?" Peggy asked.

"By six."

"In the morning?"

"The boat leaves at 6:15," Jan said. "But we need to be there early to see a video. And we have to put our wetsuits on." She pushed her empty salad plate to the side.

"*I'm* not going swimming. People can just stay on the boat, right?"

Jan blinked at her daughter. "You're not going in the water?"

"Do you know how cold that water is?"

"72°."

Peggy nodded. "That's pretty damn cold."

"That's why you wear a wetsuit."

"Yeah, I know." Peggy leaned back against the booth and folded her arms across her chest. "But I'm just not that interested. This is *your* deal."

Jan shrugged. "Suit yourself."

The mustard sauce on the grouper was a little too spicy for Peggy, but she managed to eat around it. Jan proclaimed her own meal "scrumptious," and Peggy watched, faintly envious, as her mother made steady progress through the fried shrimp, scallops and onion rings, just the sort of food she herself couldn't tolerate, not anymore; she wouldn't sleep a wink.

As Peggy and Jan were leaving the restaurant, a family came streaming in: an exhausted-looking couple with three children and an infant. The baby was crying.

"Glad we missed that," Peggy said. She pushed the door open for her mother and they stepped into the cool night air; fortunately it wasn't raining and the breeze had died down. A few stars twinkled.

"Isn't it odd," Peggy said, "that we both had just one child?" She paused, but Jan said nothing. "What was *your* reason?"

"You were enough, I guess."

"I was enough? What does *that* mean?"

Jan sighed. "Criminy, Peggy. It doesn't mean a thing."

They walked the rest of the way in silence. It would have been nice, Peggy thought, if her mother had said something tender, or at least shown a little interest in the conversation. But that wasn't her way, never had been. Not that she'd been remiss as a provider; she just wasn't keen on showing affection. Peggy's father had been the demonstrative one, freely giving hugs and praise, making up pet names that made his daughter laugh.

Peggy considered her own child. Ben was thirty-one now and living in San Diego, where he designed "green homes" and lived with a man named Tyler, to whom he was married. Which was fine. She had no problem with that, and neither did Philip. Ben was a sweet boy, everyone said so—you couldn't do better than that. And yes, she reflected now, Ben had been enough. Which was one thing, at least, that she and her mother had in common.

When they walked into the hotel lobby, a young man at the desk looked up at them and smiled. "Have a nice evening," he said. Jan paused and started to say something, but the words didn't come, and after a few seconds she closed her mouth and simply smiled at him.

"Thank you," Peggy said. "You too." She and Jan got on the elevator, and Peggy murmured, "It's okay, mom. It's no big deal." Jan did not look up.

"Do you need anything?" Peggy asked when they reached their rooms.

"I'm fine," said Jan. She pushed her card through the lock and over her shoulder said, "Sleep well, dear."

Peggy walked into her room and leaned back against the door for a moment. How strange. How strange that her mother could say that just now, yet not be able to answer the desk clerk. It happened most often, she realized, with strangers, though Jan had never been a shy woman—quiet, yes, but never shy.

Peggy felt tears welling up. What must her mother be thinking right now? She pictured her sitting on the edge of the bed, eyes open wide. Horrible, Peggy thought. Horrible to be a victim of your own mind, to sit there wondering when it would strand you and for how long.

An hour later, when she was watching TV, Peggy's stomach began to bother her—the butter sauce, foreign fish? There was no way of knowing what would give her trouble these days. The episodes were frequent now and made her feel old.

Incredibly, she'd forgotten to pack Tums—maybe her mother had something in her purse. She picked up the phone and called her room, but there was no answer. Was she in the bathroom? Peggy waited five minutes and called again, let the phone ring several times. Alarmed, she hurried out of the room and knocked on Jan's door. No answer. This made no sense; her mother was a night owl, and even more so as she'd gotten older.

Okay. She would go downstairs to see if the desk clerk had seen her. If not, she'd get him to open up the room. Heart beating wildly, Peggy took the elevator to the lobby and was on her way to the front desk when she heard a piano. She looked to the right and saw the etched glass doors to the lounge. Peggy paused a second, then strode across the carpet and entered the bar. There was just a handful of people enjoying the music, and she saw her mother right away: a small slight woman with a silver ponytail, lightly tapping her foot to a lively rendition of "I've Got You Under My Skin." She was sitting alone, and there was a drink, another Manhattan, in front of her.

Peggy's first thought was to join her, but she stopped herself. If her mother had wanted to talk, she would have asked for company.

The desk clerk gave her a small package of antacids and said he hoped she felt better soon. Riding the elevator, Peggy smiled to herself, glad to give her mother this unexpected pleasure. Jan had frowned on their staying in such an expensive hotel, and it was true they would have been perfectly comfortable somewhere cheaper, but you don't find pianists at Howard Johnson.

Manatee Gardens had a tidy office with cream-colored walls and sturdy blue awnings. There were no trapped reptiles inside, as Peggy had imagined, but there was a beautiful aquarium containing all sorts of flamboyant marine life. Peggy was glad she'd made reservations, as the 6:15 tour was filled to capacity. There were three covered pontoon boats, each designed for twelve guests.

The video was short and informative. The trip to the dive area would take ten minutes, and they would be snorkeling in about ten feet of water. In-water tour guides would be photographing the highlights of the experience, and a CD of these photos would be available for purchase. There were basic rules to follow regarding behavior in the water. Guests were NEVER to chase or crowd a manatee, or come between a mother and calf. Interrupting a sleeping or feeding manatee was forbidden, as was excessive splashing and noise. Guests were instructed to float on the surface and avoid dangling their feet and stirring up the bottom, and if they did get to touch a manatee they could only do so with one open hand. Personal wetsuits could be used, but scuba gear was prohibited as manatees were bothered by bubbles. Extra wetsuits could be found onboard in case those who declined them changed their minds. Jan nodded here and there as they watched the video; she had already seen it, she whispered, online.

Peggy and Jan were assigned to the first boat, along with four children, one teenage girl, two young mothers, two middle-aged women, and an obese, bald man—he and Peggy were the only ones who refused the snorkeling gear. The rest of them tugged on the blue and black wetsuits provided by the staff, and were then handed flippers

13

and snorkels, which they carried outside to the dock. Jan had to be fitted with a child's size suit, and though getting into it had not been easy for her, she was beaming the whole time. Peggy, walking behind her to the boats, snapped a few photos for Philip.

Captain Mike, the bearded, sandy-haired skipper in charge of their group, helped each of them onto the boat. It was still dark and chilly when they boarded, and Peggy was glad for the vinyl covering, through which she could see the moving lights of other boats and a string of brightness along the shoreline. The children were talking and giggling; the two older women were murmuring to one another, sharing comforting banalities.

Dawn broke just as they arrived at the swim site, as if this perfect timing was another detail that Manatee Gardens had carefully considered. To the east, above the dark ridge of trees, the glowing red top of the sun appeared.

"Remember, get into the water slowly," said Captain Mike. "No splashing. Let the manatees come to you."

"Where are they?" the fat man asked.

"They're down there. You'll be able to see them in a few minutes." Holding his camera, the man peered down at the water and waited.

"Oh my," said Jan, who was pulling on her flippers. She sat up and put her mask on, then looked through it at Peggy. The sight of her mother's face in those big goggles with the blue tube sticking up, made her laugh.

Sure enough, within minutes they could see into the water, could make out the sandy bottom, strewn with shells and patches of seaweed, and what they gradually began to recognize as the massive bodies of manatees, not just two or three, but a logjam of them, all hovering above the sand, their backs crusted with barnacles.

Peggy turned to Captain Mike. "How did you know they were here?"

"Secret powers," he said with a wink.

The manatees moved slowly and with odd grace, adjusting their positions with flippers that seemed too small for the job. Their fat, oblong bodies tapered to large flat paddles instead of the legs you expected to find. They looked wrong, Peggy thought, a species on the way to oblivion, unwitting, slow-moving giants not built for the world above them, the jet skis and power boats they could neither see nor avoid. They were doomed, Peggy concluded; all the coddling they required proved it.

The first one off the boat was Toby, Captain Mike's helper, who was there to take pictures and make sure no one swam too far or ran into trouble. One by one, the guests followed him into the water. Jan slipped in like a butter knife, no splash at all, and immediately she was bobbing at the surface. She gave Peggy a thumbs up, then began making her way around the boat, her silver ponytail trailing over her back. The four children streamed off like fish. The middle-aged women, who were heavy-set, required noodles for extra buoyancy.

One of the young mothers, unnerved by the size of the creatures, climbed back onto the boat after just a few minutes. Jan, on the other hand, hung in the water above a trio of manatees twice her length and several times wider. Peggy watched with apprehension, thinking about Steve Irwin and the unpredictability of wild things. What if her presence annoyed them? What if they rose up and knocked her? One little bump could crack a bone.

"Do they ever injure people?" she asked the captain. "Even unintentionally?"

He shook his head. "No ma'am. If you're gentle with them, they're gentle with you."

Peggy nodded slowly, figuring these tours had to be safe, given the potential liability.

Sunlight was flashing on the water now, and more boats could be seen moving over the bay: catamarans and pontoons, slender kayaks nosing into the tributaries. Along the tree-lined shore, streamers of lichen hung off the cypress branches and dipped into the water. Off to the right she saw a buoy that read: Closed Area – Manatee Sanctuary. They had been warned about these areas; you couldn't boat, swim, dive or fish in them. People were trying, Peggy thought, doing what they could to make up for themselves. Her gaze swept across the expanse of water, from one end of King's Bay to the other. What a lovely place it was, with the light green water and brightly colored kayaks. It was like something out of a fairy tale, all the little islands and inlets, and just a few feet below, at our mercy, those huge improbable beasts.

When Peggy looked back at her mother, she saw her face to face with a manatee, its whiskered snout nosing her goggles. Jan placed her open hand on its head, and they stayed that way a moment, before the creature slowly rolled over and offered up its belly, which Jan obligingly stroked. It was a communion beyond words, simply a way of being in the world, as honestly as anyone could be.

Language was often the first to go, Philip had said. In time, Jan's memory would fail, would start to break apart.

But not today. Today she was safe. They all were.

Peggy walked up to the captain. "I want to swim," she said.

Jean Ryan, a 2014 Lambda finalist in Lesbian General Fiction, lives in Napa, California. Her stories and essays have appeared in a variety of journals, including Other Voices, Pleiades, The Summerset Review, The Massachusetts Review *and* The Blue Lake Review. *Nominated for several Pushcart Prizes, she has also published a novel,* Lost Sister. *Her debut collection of short stories,* Survival Skills, *was published in April 2013 by Ashland Creek Press. 'Manatee Gardens' has previously appeared in* Blue Lake Review. *Please visit Jean's website at http://jean-ryan.com/*

THE HARDINESS ZONES

David Masello

S omething happened at Johnny's memorial service that I was never able to speak about with anyone else who had been there. The
other people gathered that day in Johnny's living room—which had
become his death room—are no longer friends or acquaintances.
Sometimes, these many years later, I question the occurrences of that
day and wonder if I've invented details.

But I wrote down the events, exactly as they happened and with
no embellishing, as soon as I got home that night, because I knew
that someday I would begin to doubt them. Part of me fears meeting
Johnny's parents again, though they're likely no longer alive, or any
of the other guests from the day because they might deny what I still
remember about that final visit Johnny paid us.

I've recently thought again about that visit—or whatever it should
be called—because I've begun a new job where I could have fulfilled
Johnny's greatest professional desire, been able to give him the work
he needed and wanted when we had been friends and that would
have made him happy. Not that Johnny was ever the kind of person
who seemed unhappy, even when he first got the diagnosis, days after

having collapsed on the street during a march in D.C. I remembered first hearing about that episode, getting a call in the cubicle at the magazine for which I was then working as a junior editor and someone telling me they thought Johnny was "sick"—oh, that simple term of the time that told you everything you needed to know. A word that was both a euphemism and a statement of fact.

When I spoke to Johnny a week or so later on the phone, he told me that it was true.

"Yep, I have it," he told me with an eerie confidence, a disconcerting enthusiasm—and this was eons before there was any hope of a cure, let alone an understanding of what it was or who did what to deserve it or even how *it* found its way into the body. The way he announced the news to me was that feature-writer side of him reporting to me, the editor, and others, what that collapse on K Street had meant. Johnny was an insatiable researcher on whatever topic he was assigned to write about and, well, he had gotten the information he needed on what would be his final assignment—one he did not write about.

Len, Johnny's surviving partner—though he would die a year later—greeted each guest at the memorial service. He had decided to hold the event in the room not only where Johnny had died but also beside the mattress on which he had done his dying. Most of the people who attended the service had seen Johnny in that bed. I hadn't.

For this "Celebration of Life" event, so the printed invitation had read, the bed had been neatly made, with the sheet and thin blanket and blue quilt wrapped about the mattress as precisely as if it were a birthday present. The way the blanket had been pulled back a quarter of the way and folded across made it look like a giant stripe of ribbon. Pushed against the wall, the bed surface appeared as a taut, flat expanse, a kind of featureless landscape; there were no pillows at the head. There was no box spring or frame, so the mattress seemed inordinately far away and low. It was just a piece of furniture in the high-ceilinged floor-through apartment. But everyone who entered the room—the parlor floor of a mid-19th-century townhouse—scanned the expanse of bedding looking for *something* that indicated Johnny's presence: a wrinkle in the quilt, an indentation at the center indicating the negative of his tall, slim body, a shadow-like head imprint on the white wall where he would have propped himself, reading.

On the day of the memorial service, Len was sick with bacterial pneumonia, one of the newest of a growing lexicon of ailments in the city at that time.

"But it's not contagious," he announced the moment a guest arrived and heard the cough, the congestion, saying it as if it were something as innocuous as a case of indigestion. Despite his efforts to be affectionate with everyone, most people, like me, turned their heads far from his face during the embrace, holding their breath until being released from his still-strong arms.

I knew this apartment well. Years before that service for Johnny, Len had cooked me many dinners at the place, situated on a gritty, shadeless block of West 44th Street—at least, that's how Hell's Kitchen was then. Actually, the block looks the same now, though we're all supposed to now call the neighborhood Clinton. I'm not one of those New Yorkers who misses the "edge" the city had in the '80s. It was a meaner, more dangerous, graffitied place then, but because it was the only city we knew, the one we had all arrived into and adopted after college, it's what we learned to negotiate. It's what New York was and you either endured it or you left.

Those days, you'd leave a certain bar, and you'd take a certain route home—not the more convenient one that passed the projects or the SROs where they'd throw bottles down on you. You took the E train but not the C at night. Never the G through Brooklyn. Didn't even flirt with the idea of cutting through Morningside Park, and on Monday mornings at the office, you'd hear a colleague at the coffee machine relate his or her tale of having been broken into that weekend. That kind of thing.

Len, who had "retired" at the age of 40 from the Monte Carlo Ballet, was reinventing himself as a playwright when I first met him. He had hired me to paint the apartment—it's how we met. It was one of many weekend jobs I did when I first arrived in the city and wasn't yet able to pay my rent with what I earned as an editorial assistant at Simon and Schuster. I couldn't be sure that the coat of oyster gray I saw on the walls on that evening dedicated to Johnny was the same one I had applied years earlier. I was 22 when I met Len and as I scraped the walls early Saturday mornings and rolled on the paint, which when applied sounded like two people kissing, their mutual click of saliva, I developed what felt like a love for him. Funny, then I used to like older men. Now I'm the older man, no matter what.

But after the third weekend on the job, at which point Len had shifted from my employer to a new friend, I admitted this to him, my romantic interest, my desire. I even unfolded a poem I had written about him—about how my continued scraping and torching away of the century-plus layers of paint and wallpapers kept taking us back in time together. When I asked if we could become a couple, he kindly said to me, as I stood on the highest rung of the ladder dabbing at some molded plaster ivy, "I think we need to keep things as they are. Nothing should jeopardize our friendship."

He lifted the cuff of my blue jeans and lightly kissed the back of my leg, a recognition. Not that he was ever tempted by me, physically. Len was a beautiful ballet dancer who could win the likes of a Johnny. He'd even been involved with Nureyev, who, at some later point I suddenly thought, after Nureyev died, might have been the source of it all.

Len's romantic rejection of me was my first as a real adult, someone who had moved away from my home in Illinois to begin life in New York.

When the paint job was finished after several weekends, Len celebrated by inviting me over for dinner. It would be the first of a routine we established, whereby, whenever he completed a new one-act play, he would invite me over to read the script, while he cooked us a dinner—sporadically looking over his shoulder to gauge my reactions to his writing. The plays were always short enough for me to complete before the meal was ready to be put on the table. We would discuss the play over the meal. Even though I was many years younger, Len respected my opinions, recognizing me as a writer and a young editor who knew more about such matters than he. And yet, I can't remember a single line of dialogue or plotline from one of his plays. Certainly, he'd never have imagined the real-life one that developed. Who could? Unless you wrote science fiction.

One evening, early on in our new friendship, Len told me that the building in which he lived was one of New York's official haunted houses. The steep-stooped, four-story Italianate townhouse had been built in 1860, maybe even earlier, on the site of an apple orchard in which a wife had killed her adulterous husband, and she, or both of them, had yet to vacate the premises—so went the tale. A fellow tenant on another floor confirmed this story for me, but she insisted that the image of *another* former resident of the building, Gypsy Rose Lee, appeared some evenings in the vestibule mirror, adjusting sequins on her dress and patting her sprayed confection of hair, even applying some makeup. The tenant had said that before she could reach the point on the staircase where she would be able to see Miss Lee in full, perhaps even greet her, the long-deceased star of the burlesque would vanish—as if, like a hologram, her image depended on a precise viewing angle.

But the first time this tale of the house being haunted had real meaning for me, firsthand, was at one of those play-date dinners on a winter night, just a couple of years before Len and Johnny met and Johnny moved in. On that evening, I remember watching Len in the nearby kitchen stooping to take a roast out of the oven when a squat log that had been snapping in the fireplace suddenly rolled with propelled momentum out and into the room. It was as if it had been pushed—it moved with that much force. The piece of wood actually rolled over the brick lip of the fireplace, defying gravity. And as it did so, the pine-floor planks in the room caught fire immediately, the flames running the lengths of the boards as if following fuses. I grabbed a broom and began to beat the ankle-high flames, but the straw caught fire and I had to throw it out a window. Len meanwhile ran into the bathroom and from the tub filled a wastebasket, heaving load after load of water into the room and onto the floor. The hissing log, which had rolled all the way across the room, was soon rendered as inert as driftwood. Curly black flakes of ash sloshed in the room's charred corners, like a shallow apron of surf, and a gray cloud of smoke hovered.

Johnny and I became closer friends after he and I had both decided to try freelance writing at the same time. He quit his staff job at a downtown alternative newsweekly where he wrote features and essays about men's fashion and urban culture. This was a time in the city when Avenue A was treated like a DMZ and you could stop in at nearly a dozen bookstores along Fifth Avenue from 57th Street to 42nd. My focus as a freelancer was less defined—writing articles about architecture, book reviews of first novels, and features for glossy shelter magazines about the interiors of houses I never visited. For those stories, I simply interviewed, over the phone, the decorators and the occupants of the homes. The decorators always said the same phrases, as if they thought they were being original: "The place was a wreck when we began our work, but it had good bones." "My design philosophy is that I like to mix the old with the new." "I prefer a neutral palette with pops of color."

For moral support during the often silent, idle, workless afternoons, Johnny and I would sometimes meet at Caffé Dante on MacDougal Street, where the only patrons mid-afternoon, weekdays, were retired Italian men who gathered there after games of bocce and a pair of elderly widows who always shared a powdered-sugar-dusted canola and carefully reapplied lipstick after they had finished their cup of espresso.

In trying to figure out what it was we really wanted to write, Johnny had surprised me one day by saying, while stirring sugar into his cappuccino, "If I could write about anything, all of the time, it would be gardens. What it's like to occupy them, to walk the paths, how they're designed, how people tend them, why people grow them. I don't think that would ever bore me."

One of the several columns I now edit at yet another big glossy magazine is the monthly gardening feature, a subject for which I am incapable of evincing any enthusiasm or retaining knowledge that takes metaphorical root. I can't remember the cultivar from the specimen name or grasp the meaning of the U.S. hardiness zones—something about parts of the country where you can grow certain things, where plants will thrive, or not. I look at a map of those zones put out by the Department of Agriculture listing average temperatures and rainfall, but the moment I try to make sense of it, the shaded portions just blur into a kind of Impressionistic wash of colors. I don't know exactly why gardening doesn't interest me, but I think some of it has to do with its ephemeral nature. Things grow, they bloom, then they die, with no record of their having existed. And apart from trees, nothing lasts that long. Same with writing about interior design—most of those interiors are staged for the photo shoot and what's there can change later that day. Yet, I am now in charge of creating every gardening story in the magazine and assigning it to a writer. Were Johnny alive, I would make him our regular columnist, include his name on the masthead, and give him a contract. With his passion for the subject, coupled with his talent as a writer, I wouldn't have to worry about that column. It would likely be the easiest part of my job.

This anecdote about Johnny's desire to write about gardens—this piece of his history—is what I wanted to talk about that evening when Len asked us all if we had remarks to share before we performed a farewell toast for Johnny in the room. To present a mini eulogy, I guess. The twenty-or-so of us had assembled into a large, uneven circle, an ellipse, I suppose you could call it. We were all standing. As people recounted their memories of their friendship with Johnny, the ring was sporadically broken as someone pivoted outward and bent to wipe away tears, reminding me of those old carnival shooting galleries of ducks. Too many years have passed for me to remember anything anyone said about Johnny. He was 25 when he died. How much could you say about someone's life at that point?

I said nothing to the assembled crowd about Johnny and his love of gardens, not because I was nervous about speaking in front of them or losing my composure, but because I hadn't earned the right to do so. I never visited Johnny once he became bedridden and, so, I felt like a fraud, a peripheral, ghostly friend who had only conveyed regards and concern through mutual-friend mediums. I hadn't seen Johnny in this room in the bed on the floor. I had only heard second-hand about his physical changes.

True, I had invited him to a cocktail party at my apartment on 11th Street, shortly before he took to the bed fulltime. On the evening of my party, Johnny buzzed me from the foyer of my tenement building. I lived on the fifth floor, a classic, early 20th-century "dumbbell" walkup. I buzzed him in, but realized fifteen minutes later while attending to my guests that he had yet to arrive at my door. I went into the hallway and started to walk down the stairs when I found him on the fourth-floor landing, drenched in sweat, gripping the handrail to get his breath. His once-blond hair had dulled and was limp. That limpness, lack of body and color and sheen in the hair, usually accompanied by a snowfall of dandruff on the shoulders, was just one of those symptoms everyone had. As if the physical body was grabbing at every bit of protein it could find. His cheeks and forehead appeared dented, like the hollowed-out faces you see on well-preserved mummies. We locked arms and I accompanied him, creaking step-by-step, that final level up and into my party.

Johnny stayed at the party a short time. When he told me he
needed to leave, I escorted him to the staircase, patted him on
his back, and coaxed him on to begin the descent. I talked to
him through the rectangular stairwell opening during his entire
trip down, a chorus of cooing pigeons accompanying us from the
airshaft. At each landing, he stopped to get his breath. The tenement's skylight, a jigsaw puzzle of netted panes, hovered over us
like a gray cloud, not so unlike that one from smoke in Len's apartment during that floor fire. Finally, Johnny reached the bottom. I
looked down onto the top of his head, as small as a boy's. He didn't
look up. He raised his right arm straight up into the air and bade
farewell by turning his hand in a back-and-forth corkscrew motion, akin to the way Queen Elizabeth waves. It was my last sighting
of him alive.

I had other friends at the same time who were as gravely ill as Johnny,
but they were mostly older; their situations were, somehow, more
bearable. Their lives were filled with sex with strangers, whereas
Johnny and Len were a faithful couple, from what I had heard. If it
happened to them, none of us were safe. Those older friends, I could
visit—as if their age and their behavior had made the illness inevitable. But Johnny, mid-twenties, was too handsome to see dying, if
such a thing is possible to say. He was akin to some doomed, smooth-
skinned World War I poet who foresaw his death, whose final rhym-
ing couplets would be found tucked into his helmet.

Early in the memorial service gathering, I met Johnny's grand-
mother, Sarah—energetic, smiling, looking at me through sparkling
wire-rim glasses, like a fervent suffragette.

"I am so happy Johnny has died," she said to me.

I was shocked by the remark, and must have shown it, until she
continued, "He suffered so badly, as you, one of his closest friends,

must know. And now, well, he's free of all that. *That's* what I meant, dear."

"And in a way, even that was odd," she added, "because Johnny loved being a writer and a reporter and just about everything a person can get with this he got—no experience about the disease was denied him. He didn't seem to be immune to anything. He eagerly researched each of his new ailments as if he were writing an article. The reality of it was his primary source."

The moment for the final toast had come. Everyone had said what they intended. Standing on either side of me were Johnny's parents, who had driven in from Princeton, where he had been born and was now buried. Guests had spoken of the funeral service and described the long line of people who had gathered along Nassau Street. I had not been one of them; I had not been invited, nor had I deserved to be.

"We're going to say, 'To Johnny,'" Len instructed us. "We'll say it in unison. We'll raise our glasses of wine, say it, then take a sip."

We followed his instructions. And, so, at the very moment those words, "To Johnny!" were shouted, as if we were a Greek chorus, each of us pinching the stem of our glass held high in the air, the chandelier in the room dimmed. All the way down. I remember each crystal droplet losing its light, fading from a radiant, cheerful yellow brightness, to a Victorian rosiness then, to, to nothing, the ceiling's plaster acanthus leaves and bas-reliefed serpentine vines darkening into shadows, withering away from sight, their details lost.

Johnny's mother swung around to the room's dimmer switch to find no one there, her string of pearls clattering as they whipped against her neck. She spun with such force that one of her clip-on earrings flew off, ricocheting against a wall. She turned to me and she whispered in a tone that held both panic and hope, "Could it be?"

"How could it not?" I said, as I bent to retrieve her earring.

When I handed it to her, she pinched the gold orb between two fingers but didn't reapply it to her ear. Rather, she stood in place and looked off into that middle distance, that destination we all see when the present is not where we want to be.

A couple of the guests wandered to the room's dimmer switch and spun the dial, drawing their faces close to it, as if looking for a mechanical failure, a loose screw, snapped spring, something practical, a reason. To them, this was about a simple electrical shortage, a manmade flaw. For others of us, those who stood holding our glass of wine, looking to the bed, the chandelier, it seemed that there was another explanation.

So, even in that room of people, unified by our love for Johnny, there was a divide of beliefs, neither stated, just enacted. For those who registered the dimming as something electrical, a coincidence of current, I felt a kind of disdain.

Johnny's death—and Len's—came at the latter end of it all, when suddenly there was some kind of hope, a mix of drugs and therapies. Early on, 1985, or so, I attended a cocktail party at the Upper East Side mansion owned by Matilde Krim, then one of the leading researchers and spokespersons, and her husband, a Hollywood producer. She had already become a kind of hero for me, with her measured responses and ever-calm comments about the disease on television shows and in *Times* articles. At the party, when I asked her outright whether there would ever be a cure, whether there would ever come a time when I wouldn't be afraid, she said, in her elegant German-Swiss accent, "Science will solve this."

Her words felt oracular, sage-like. They comforted me and I intoned them regularly for years when I would be afraid. Yet, there was a bit of peril in those words, too—when *would* that solution be found? In our lifetime? My lifetime? Would science follow its natural course of death until there were no more deaths to be had?

And, in many ways, she was right. Science has solved some of it and had begun to do so very soon after Johnny's death. Had he survived just a little longer, been that much hardier, maybe he would be alive today, middle-aged, as I. Len would be an elderly man now.

The work I do as an editor of a magazine continues on. That gardening column is written by a rotating series of freelancers I hire, not one of whom is a good writer, though they know the subject well. There is not a moment of what I might call poetry in their prose, just factual, unimaginative copy, absent any writerly nuance, about such subjects as proper fertilizing techniques, pruning, the planting of borders of ivy.

Not unlike that subject matter of gardening, magazine editing is a seasonal endeavor, too. You are always planning months ahead, never living in the one now. Come summer, you are already on to the garden in winter; spring and you are thinking about the decay of fall. For those who cultivate gardens, plants and flowers go in and out of bloom, so that for seasons at a time, you forget what grew where, but when they sprout again, you remember.

David Masello is a widely published essayist, feature writer, and poet. He is a longtime magazine editor and writer, having held senior editorial positions at Town & Country, Art & Antiques, Travel & Leisure, Departures, *and other periodicals. He was the founding editor-in-chief of* Out Traveler. *He is currently executive editor of* Milieu, *a magazine about design. Prior to his magazine work, he was a hardcover nonfiction editor at Simon and Schuster. He is the author of two books about architecture and art. He has published in the* New York Times, Salon, Boston Globe, *and other periodicals and anthologies, including* Best American Essays.

THE TRACKS

Lee Lynch

Well, I made it, thought Augusta Brennan, with a peaceful sigh as she slumped against the lace doily on the back of her easy chair. She couldn't believe she survived a convalescent home, but here she was, settled in her tiny house, her old cat Mackie hauling himself into a leap for her lap. They sat, the housekeeping done.

The morning sun warmed her self-cut, shaggy white hair. It was sometimes a bit dirty because positioning herself at the sink to wash it was hard. Her face was hot with a flush that increased from exertion and excitement. She squinted at the bright window, watching for activity on the street, inquisitive always and eager to be outside soon; her stout body looked as if it had grown padding from every blow life dealt her.

"You didn't think I'd come back, did you, Mackie?" she said and chuckled. After sixteen years she knew just how to stroke him behind the ears and Mackie purred. "Thank goodness for Karen and Jean. If they hadn't taken you in, it might not have been worth my while to get well." She survived for Mackie and to return to her one-of-a-kind perfect home.

Built between railroad tracks and a street, hers was the last in a row of narrow houses an enterprising builder had been able to squeeze onto a tapering piece of land. At first Gussie feared she wouldn't even have room to turn around, but the girls reassured her and took charge of arranging her furniture. The lack of space outweighed the cheap rent.

She surveyed her realm above a contented Mackie. Its shape reminded her of water wings, those old inflated rubber contraptions she used at the beach when she was young. The two swollen sides of the apartment, one containing bedroom and bath, the other sitting room and kitchenette, were connected by the narrow neck of a foyer, closet and front door.

In these rooms she made her home, sunlight playing on the colors of her favorite possessions like musical notes in a song of her life. It shone on her tri-colored afghan, on some small braided rugs the girls got her at a rummage sale, on her mother's faded quilt, which lay warm and soft and enormous across her daybed.

Her little stone house by the railroad tracks was homey now. She puttered in it just like an old lady, she told herself. The convalescent home was cold like a weak winter sun. While there, she'd wrapped herself in her afghan and watched the little girls play across the street in the schoolyard, remembering and remembering. Now she hardly had the time to remember; this little place took an awful lot of housework. Or maybe she wasn't as speedy as she'd once been.

An engine pulled a box car past the house. "It must be 10:00," she said to Mackie. "Time to go across the street to the market." Nan, her next door neighbor, was coming to lunch. "Shall I get you a special treat?" In answer, Mackie yawned.

It was a strain, having a guest. Between the shopping, preparing food, the visit itself, cleaning and resting up afterwards, a whole day would be gone. A whole day in her dwindling number of days. When her time had been plentiful she would squander it, wishing it shorter if her job was boring or she had something painful to live through.

No more; she hoarded every minute. The trains reminded her how fast her days slipped away. Most old folks, she thought, would be bothered by the regular racket of the trains, but she'd grown up next to tracks used much more than these, long before cars took over.

She and Nan talked a lot about how they hated cars. Neither had ever driven the dangerous machines which flung themselves across the country, getting everyone where they didn't need to be faster than they needed to get there. Karen and Jean spoke of the way the automobile and trucking industries used their power and riches to weaken the rail system, just as she saw cars weakening the old ways of life. Now the sound of the trains was like the lowing of the last buffalo on the western plains. Trains were yet another idea men rejected in order to make more money.

Gussie closed her eyes to the sun. She was starting to think like the girls. Next thing she knew she'd be marching with them.

Mackie purred louder when she switched to his other ear. Here was the 10:21 freight train. It would be a long time rumbling by. She'd better get ready to go out.

As she rose, Mackie leapt down. He strolled to a window where, between trains, birds gathered to peck at the crumbs she put on the sill. The train ran on and on. She moved to the window where she kept her knickknacks. She'd tried to hang a shelf for them, but her knuckles were too stiff. Holding a hammer was an awkward exercise that produced cracks and gashes and one sore thumb. The girls would help and then Mackie could add this window to his collection of lounging ledges.

She'd arranged everything symmetrically: plants in twin white pots, new cuttings in old shot glasses, a miniature framed cat portrait, a little watering can, and several tiny figurines purchased in five-and-ten-cent stores across the U.S. From outside, she thought the accumulation must look like an old lady's treasures, fit for nothing when she died but to be thrown away. To her, this window was a joy, full of suggestions of loves, of thriving life, of color. The way all the objects crowded on the windowsill gave her a sense of a life bursting at the seams with travel, women, new beginnings. And loss—poor years too, times when life had been difficult to take, but, as a cutting might not make it, or as a plant that was pruned grew on, so her life continued with its bustling shoots and blossoms around the cuts and failures.

She thought of the blossoming of women in the night as trains sped by. So many lovely women, lovely nights. The thought of women reminded her of Nan and she'd best get to the store or Nan would be left on the doorstep waiting for her lunch. She went to the closet in the neck of the house, drew a light coat over her sweater and slacks, picked her big black purse off the doilied table, and locked the door carefully behind her.

Earlier in her hurried life her surroundings had often been a blur, but now she walked slowly, sat long hours, and was learning the art of looking and appreciating what she saw. She was grateful she still had her sight. She held onto the rough gray stone of the house as she made her way down its steps.

She passed Nan's house and peered up at the windows, but there was no sign of her neighbor. Nan owned her narrow home and lived there over forty years with her husband. She had no worries but where the tax money would come from and she fretted that to death, annoying Gussie at times. Gussie told her to take in a boarder.

"Some old coot I'd have to take care of?" Nan had sounded cross. "I can barely take care of myself. I'm seventy-seven!"

She went by the travel agency. Often, she stopped to read the posters. A couple of big old rooming houses came next, where the tracks veered farther from the road. Then the little luncheonette where she sometimes went with Nan. As she crossed to the store, she admired the red stone fire station whose towers and cool, gasoline and oil smells made her heart race almost as fast as it had when she was a little girl. How she had wanted to be a fireman!

Aside from the scenery, her trip to the store was uneventful. She carried her luncheon meat, quart of milk and small jar of mayonnaise in a net shopping bag. The sun was always a little higher in the sky on the way back, and she was always a little more tired than when she went out. A cup of tea, a short rest and she'd be fine when Nan arrived.

But she still felt depleted after her rest and slowly made sandwiches, cutting the crusts from white bread, tossing scraps of meat to Mackie as he purred and rubbed against her legs. The last luncheon she prepared, a couple of weeks back, had been for Jean and Karen. She made them tuna fish. Like so many of these young lesbians, they wouldn't eat mammal flesh, wouldn't smoke or drink. These were things she never needed in abundance, living the simple life she had, but still, without drinking, without smoking, without eating in restaurants, what kind of fun did they have? No wonder they got into so many emotional messes with each other. Their world was so small, filled only by themselves, friends just like them, and an old lady they seemed to think had drifted down from the moon.

Their fascination at meeting a lesbian in her eighties still lingered. They asked questions all the time: How do you handle this? Did you have a lot of lovers? All at once? Were you ever committed to just one woman?" Questions, questions, questions! As if their lives hadn't been so similar that, transplanted to her time, they probably would have lived very much as she had.

"There," she told Mackie as she set the pink glass plates with their sandwiches on a shelf in the refrigerator. She supposed she should cover them with waxed paper, decided they would keep till Nan arrived.

She had to economize in small ways or her money would be depleted. With clumsy fingers, she emptied a tray of ice cubes into the tea pitcher and refilled the tray with water, then wiped the spills. She set the table with her best cloth napkins and silverware.

Out back of the house, on a tiny strip of land fenced from the tracks, she'd noticed a smattering of wildflowers. She went to pick some for the table, but stooping, got dizzy and walked unsteadily, with darkened sight, back toward her door, wildflowers drooping from her left hand, while with her right she felt her way along the cool stones of the house.

"Augusta!" cried Nan on her way from next door. "Are you all right?" Nan hurried to her, in that broad-shouldered, long-legged, yet timid way she had.

"I will be in a minute." Her words came out in a growl that surprised her. "Here, take these darned flowers. They were meant to pretty up the table for our lunch, but I see now I wasn't meant to pick that particular bunch."

"How many times have I told you about stooping? You're just like my husband; he would not listen to me and exerted himself every way he could until he killed himself doing it. I won't have that happen to you."

She never could decide if Nan blamed herself or Mr. Heimer for his death—he'd been mowing their tiny patch of grass under a hot sun—or even whether Nan really minded that she was finally alone in her home.

Nan was taller than most women of her generation and bent like a tree under a constant wind of anticipated disapproval. She had a plain face, so unmarked by age that Gussie wondered if there had been more character in it when Nan was young. Eventually she realized it was this very plainness coupled with her height that led Nan to a life where she could avoid the pains and rejections that line faces. Given money and good circumstances she might have been raised a "lady," but she became, instead, a girl forced to find her own protections. Nan found them in a husband who kept her home, childless, until the war, when she reemerged to work until there were calluses on her hands and a certain courage that kept her from retreating entirely into her home.

Still, the world's early imprint was in that stoop and in a way she had of not looking into Gussie's eyes. But Nan's smile, when it came, was broad and unafraid, and laughter was something she easily shared. Her hair was still brown, in feathery short curls fluffed up all over her head, and she wore thick glasses. Nan's shy safe home was sacred to her. She sometimes fretted. "What will I do if I go blind?"

Gussie never answered her, not wanting to be presumptuous. Someday, she thought, Nan would figure it out, though Gussie would miss her own water wing of a home. Meanwhile, she enjoyed watching that strangely young face soften in her presence.

They walked inside with care and Gussie lowered herself to her chair while Nan went to the kitchen for a glass of water. Mackie lumbered up to her lap. The poor old boy looked so concerned she nuzzled with him.

"Like a couple of old lovebirds, you are," said Nan and handed Gussie her water.

"He's worried."

"How can you tell?"

"All this attention he's giving me."

"Humph," Nan said. Was she jealous? "Are you better?"

"Yes, much better. Thank you for your help. I'll sit a moment before I get lunch out."

"Why don't you let me? Knowing you, it's all ready."

"But –"

"Why not? We've done this enough. I know where everything is."

"You're my guest."

"And you've been mine. I already know how good a hostess you are. It seems to me," Nan said, leaning close to Gussie and looking her in the eye for once, "that it's about time we treated each other like friends rather than old ladies come visiting."

Gussie knew her face was reddening around a delighted smile.

Nan reddened too, and looked quickly to the floor, as if someone else entirely had been speaking so frankly.

"Well, then, why don't you move out to the kitchen and serve us lunch!"

"Yes, ma'am," Nan said with a teasing salute.

Gussie knew Nan had greatly enjoyed her war work. The military atmosphere had replaced many of the civilian conventions that made her shy. Not to mention the strictly female environment. Gussie herself had been called "Sarge" back then. As accountant, she'd taken over many of the men's managerial tasks. This new authority, combined with her commanding stride, had inspired the nickname. She and Nan fell into their wartime personas easily.

They ate in the cool parlor, Gussie with her feet up, Mackie pleading for scraps with his green eyes and an occasional flick of his tail, and Nan relaxed, listening to Gussie's stories of the morning. "Gussie," Nan said, "you can make a story of anything, even a walk across the street to the store."

Meal done, the two friends sat in silence for a while. An occasional annoying car sped along the street, while silence hung over the railroad tracks. The sound of the present was, for the moment, louder than that of the past. Gussie dwelt on what Nan said about their relationship. It made her nervous to be getting this close to a woman after years of being without a lover or close friend. She always assumed old people didn't begin new relationships and hadn't expected this.

But before they could go any deeper, she would have to reveal her past, and she didn't know how Nan felt about lesbians. She wondered if Nan had ever questioned her own life and how she was living it. She wondered if Nan would condemn the way Gussie lived hers.

Despite her concern, there was a pervading air of comfort in the parlor. She was reminded of two old men who'd lived in her town when she was young. Their habit, as a matter of fact, had been to sit together outside the fire station evenings, just inside if it rained. They'd been friends all their lives and though you seldom saw them exchange a word, you knew that the act of sitting together, smoking cigars, was one of great intimacy, respect, even love. She must mention this to Karen and Jean—how when she thought of friendship between old people, she thought of the two men.

The little 2:00 p.m. passenger train went quickly north past her window. Five minutes later a train to the city slowed toward the station half a mile down the road. Mackie slept on the window sill, snoring, two legs hanging over the edge.

She said, "I've been thinking of trains a lot lately, Nan. Every time I hear one it seems I remember something from my past. Trains meant a lot more then. They were a way of life and we children would become terribly excited when they ran through town on the way to big cities, to the coasts, to anywhere we'd never been. We often played along the tracks and could tell a train was on its way from vibrations in the ground. We'd stop whatever we were doing to watch it and wave with such vigor you'd think the train would never make its destination without us."

Nan looked up, as if she heard something in Gussie's tone. A little too much intimacy, perhaps?

Gussie said, "I found rentals near the tracks even when I could afford better." She paused; decided to go on. "New London, Connecticut, was no different.

"When I first got there and knew no one, I'd walk to the big old station on a Sunday and sit on a bench watching, maybe talk to someone waiting for a train."

Nervous, she interrupted herself. "Can I offer you a beer? Seems to me two old ladies, on a hot afternoon, might as well live it up."

"Should you?"

"Of course I should. I had a little faintness from bending over, that's all. Go ahead and get it. I hope you don't mind a quart bottle of ale." She didn't try to make herself heard while Nan was in the kitchen. "I bought it the other day, hardly realizing I was remembering New London and Violet."

Nan returned. Gussie smiled at the sight of the bottle. "Hasn't changed much in all these years." Nan looked puzzled. "I recall sitting in a tavern near the New London station, drinking ale with Violet."

She took a deep breath as Nan poured the light-gold liquid.

"When I think of New London, that's who I remember, Violet. Her father owned the factory where I did accounting. He'd started the business in his home town, Providence, Rhode Island, then built the New London plant. As he aged it got more difficult to travel. Violet was his only child and she was not planning to be anyone's housewife. She wanted to take over the business when her father retired. To prove her worth to him she came down to New London when she was needed and worked at the Providence plant.

"That's how I met her. Rain was pouring down, but I got there before it started and sat there dry as a bone watching travelers come in all bedraggled.

"Violet sat next to me, umbrella dripping, and sneezed. She said, 'Excuse me.' I said 'God bless you.' She looked at me then and recognized me from the plant.

"She took out her ticket and I saw it was for Providence. The schedule board showed her train two hours late and I waited for her to notice it. Meanwhile, I noticed her.

"She was as tall as you, thin and elegant-looking, in a competent way. Well-dressed in the latest fashion, but no frills, as if it was the thing to do and she was determined to do it well. Now, of course, she looked like she needed a change of clothes. Violet whispered a very unladylike curse under her breath; she'd seen the schedule board. I kind of smiled in sympathy toward her. She shrugged and set off for the phones, leaving her overnight bag behind. She stopped and looked at me as if to ask me to watch the bag and I made a gesture to say of course. Whoever she called, she felt better afterward. Perhaps a young husband? I had no way of knowing at the time she was not married. To a man.

"I realized the rain had stopped and rose to leave. On impulse, perhaps because she had asked me to watch her bag, I turned to her and explained I lived nearby. Would she like to change into something dry at my apartment?

"At that moment we saw the stationmaster saunter to the schedule board. Erased the 'Two' and chalked in 'Three hours late.' Violet walked home with me.

"I started to make tea, but she admitted she'd like something stronger to drink. All I had then, as now, was the ale, and that pleased her. I got glasses while she changed. There was a fresh moist smell of deluged pavement coming in through my windows and I felt moved, in a physical way, if you don't mind me saying so. The smell of summer rains always has that effect on me. Too, there was something about Violet which was very sensual."

She looked at Nan to see how she was reacting. Nan sat, as she had all along, legs stretched before her, ale in hand, a sleepy faraway look on her face as she stared away from Gussie out the window before her.

"Of course I offered to send the clothes, but she reminded me how often she came to New London and I agreed to keep them. We drank the ale and talked, in a way I hadn't been able to since I'd moved there. I enjoyed her immensely and she seemed to enjoy me. I made her a jolly little indoor picnic before she left. When she learned I worked for her father's company she seemed pleased. I never thought to say I'd bring her clothing to work with me so we agreed, when I walked her to the station under my umbrella, that she would stop at my office and tell me when she was next in town.

"She returned sooner than anticipated; the next week. I thought of her a lot in the meantime. Why not? I was lonely and she'd been so pleasing to me, somehow, like slipping into a warm bath when you ache and luxuriating in its smoothness on your skin."

Nan now watched her with what looked like curiosity.

"Violet agreed to come to supper and I put on quite the spread. She was, after all, the boss's daughter. My pleasure in her company was almost incidental to the way I would have treated her as an employer. And, you see, I thought I knew why she was all smiles when she emerged from my bedroom that first visit. I always left certain books, certain framed photographs, lying about the room. One picture in particular may have intrigued her."

Gussie fidgeted in her chair a bit, thinking how these things got no easier with age. She took a long draught of ale.

"The photo was of me and another woman. We were embracing. Kissing. A friend had taken it because she was enamored of the way we looked together and wanted to show us why."

Nan said nothing, didn't move.

She went on. She'd come this far, why not? "So, you see, I thought her smile might signal acceptance. Perhaps a kinship. I hoped to find out which that night.

"Dinner went nicely. Violet appreciated a home cooked meal. The walk we took, this time without rain, at twilight, was wonderful. When it was time for her to go I wanted her to stay with all my heart. But then, she'd given no indication that she would be interested—and she was still the boss's daughter. I wanted so much to be held by those long arms, to feel those long legs next to mine. She was, simply, the sexiest woman I'd ever met.

"'I need to go back to my room,' Violet said. 'I call Denise every night I'm away.'

"I knew this was my signal. Our kinship was real. 'Oh. There's no need to go all the way back there,' I said, pretending innocence. 'Use mine.'

"She must have known I was offering more than a telephone because she hesitated, her brows drawn, her eyes pained for a long minute before she said yes.

"And this is another reason I've been remembering New London lately. Her pain. You've seen my friends Karen and Jean." Nan nodded very slightly. "Well, half the time they arrive crying over what they're going through. This one wants to be lovers without letting the other one go, and the other is tired of being lovers with others and wants to be single, and then this one is in pain because that one

40

is in love with someone else. And on and on about how they have to go through this in order not to stifle each other, to grow and change and I don't know what all. They ask me what to do but I know they don't want to hear my answer, so I just listen to them thrash about in their pain and confusion, knowing no one can answer these kinds of questions for anyone else.

"Once in a while I tell them a bit of my own experience and they listen, oh yes, they listen, as if to some quaint fairy tale that has absolutely nothing to do with them. As if loving in my time was so very different, as if Violet did not hurt as much as they do by deciding yes, she would wrap her lovely legs around mine that night and a great many more nights while her lover off in Providence longed for her. As if I, wanting Violet so badly, being immediately seduced on that train station bench by her elegance, her sexiness, and lost, lost in the most intense desire I have ever felt for anyone, as if I could deny this to myself or proceed from reasons other than those that had grown suddenly and spontaneously in my heart."

She went silent as a freight train rolled by, unendingly. "Each time I hear a train I'm reminded of the joy of her arrivals, the sheer bliss of knowing she was walking down those wet steamy summer streets toward me, bringing the scent of travel, of railroad cars, of another city, another woman to me, bringing that long, smooth body and those hands that did such magic in the night. And, too, I am reminded of the pain of her departures. I knew she would never be mine. I knew her love for Denise was deeper, stronger, longer than her love for me, that ours would be a brief, intense love. But the sound of her train pulling out, the withdrawal of those hands from me, the exquisite sadness of it all—I cannot describe it.

"And to see those girls belabor it, think they are different with their *reasons* for what they do. In time, in time, they will decide. As Violet decided it was the long slow comfort of what she had with Denise, the rich, shared time and the common belongings, memories, friends. The familiar body in the bed, the warmth and comfort of their home. Just as I decided to pursue my heights, keep riding the trains, see all I thought I must see. I was thirsty for experience; she was hungry for substance. We both knew and accepted this, though we never talked about it. Whether she told Denise I never knew. That was their business."

She poured more ale into Nan's glass. "I suspect Jean and Karen simply don't want the consequences of their decisions. They want the heights and comforts without the pain, without having to choose or lose anything along the way. They talk it to death, beat each other over the head emotionally. What makes them act like that?"

"Cars," said Nan.

They sat in quiet, Gussie thinking how to respond. It was a hard concept to grasp and had to do with the new ways, the fast pace, the mobility cars brought. Young people were used to getting what they wanted and where they wanted fast. This generation seemed to want to take everything apart and put it together again, inside out and upside down.

Nan got up and topped off their glasses. She went into the bathroom. At her return Gussie took a turn, rising with difficulty after sitting so long. She looked at herself in the bathroom mirror, something she was usually loath to do. Her shaggy white hair had a cowlick. Her cheeks were reddened. Lines travelled like tracks to her eyes. She was numbed by the ale, and warm, and buzzing like a hive of busy little bees cooking up something she couldn't quite cook up for herself. She smiled at the face that was so good at revealing all the life still swarming inside.

"I hope my story hasn't upset you," she said when she returned to the parlor. No train passed, Mackie had abandoned the window and the street was quiet. "I needed to talk with someone my own age about what I see the girls doing. I don't know how to help them. They probably just have to live through it as we all did, but in their own way. Of course it was wrong of Violet to hide our affair from Denise, but look at the pain Jean and Karen endure for their truths."

Nan gazed her way, smiling slightly.

"Then again," Gussie said, "perhaps this is all hogwash. Just a way to tell you about myself."

The sunlight faded from the window. The sky darkened. Huge drops of rain landed in sizzling splats on the hot sidewalk. A smell of wet asphalt came through the window, a smell of wet earth, the steamy smells of a quick summer shower. The rain slowed, became quieter. She knew she should get up and close some windows.

Instead, she said, "You know, Nan, I think you're lovely."

Lee Lynch's most recent books, The Raid *and* Beggar of Love, *are published by Bold Strokes Books. Her national column is* "The Amazon Trail." *She is the namesake and first recipient of The Lee Lynch Classic Award for* The Swashbuckler. *She's been honored with the Golden Crown Literary Society Trailblazer Award, the Alice B. Reader Award, induction into the Saints and Sinners Literary Hall of Fame, the James Duggins Mid-Career Award, and, for* Beggar of Love, *the Lesbian Fiction Readers Choice Award, the Ann Bannon Popular Choice Award, and Book of the Year Award from ForeWord Reviews. In October 2014, Lynch's* An American Queer, Twenty-Five Years of The Amazon Trail *will be published by Bold Strokes.*

ARE YOU A BOY OR A GIRL?

Stephanie Mott

It is Saturday morning, and I don't have anything pressing this morning. I know from experience that this is totally the best time for me to write. My mind is free to follow its own path. Many of (what I think are) my better writings have come from sitting at this computer at this time of day on this particular day of the week.

Mr. Kitty is at my side. He has his own chair next to mine. He was five years old when I adopted him from some friends who were moving into an apartment that had rules about cats. He was not able to go with them. I was helping them load up some boxes and things. That was almost seven years ago.

I remember that day quite well. Yes, because it was the day that I became Mr. Kitty's person. But also because it was the day a four-year-old boy asked me, *Are you a boy, or are you a girl?* I responded, *That's a good question*, buying myself a few moments to think about how to answer.

I didn't look very much like a woman at the time, and I didn't exactly look like a man either. It was an awkward time in my transition, when questions like this one were just beginning to become an expected part of my day, although seldom as innocent and honest as was the question on this day.

After a few seconds, I stopped and turned to the boy and asked, *What do you think?* He stopped and looked at me and said, *I think you are a girl because you have a purse and you are wearing a necklace.* I said, *That's a good answer.* And from that moment on, I was a girl in this young man's mind. The question had been asked and answered. That was that. No need to spend any more time trying to figure out what it all meant, or if it was right or wrong. It just was.

It was during this same time in my transition that I went with some friends to a local restaurant for lunch. As I sat down at the table with my friends, I noticed some other patrons staring at me. Soon after, they caught the attention of their server and were quickly shuffled off to another table, where they wouldn't have to look at me.

Those were the days, my friend. Every moment of every day contained the possibility that anything could happen. Anything good, and anything bad. *You are so courageous to be who you are,* some people would say to me. I would respond as politely as I knew how, but I would be thinking how courageous it would be to go back to not being who I am.

Those were frightening times, but at least they contained the possibility that something good could happen. Before, that possibility didn't exist. All that existed was the certainty that each and every day would contain thoughts of suicide. The certainty that eventually I would die, and that would be the day the pain stopped. Going back to that life would have been truly courageous, indeed.

It was during this time in my transition that I was able to start my day in front of the makeup mirror. To choose the day's clothing by how it matched my soul and told the truth, rather than by how it reminded me of the daily lie of pretending to be a man.

It was a time when I walked out the door of my home in sweet, perfect honesty. A time when my closet became a place for clothing—which was a good thing because I was about to need the space.

It was a time of hope. Living in a time of hope is far less courageous than living in a time of no hope. It was a time when dreams began to become dares, and dares began to become life. It was a time when I would begin to surround myself with people who didn't need to ask if I was a boy or girl. They knew.

I began to discover myself within the framework of who I was. To discover my woman self within a newly discovered freedom to be my woman self. And watch her come to life. And see me come to life with her. As her.

Little did I know of the amazing journey that could only begin when I asked myself the same question that was asked by the four-year-old boy. Am I a boy, or am I a girl? Little did I know that there would still be otherwise knowledgeable adults, seven years later, still asking the same question.

I haven't found it necessary to ask myself the same question in a really long time. I still have a purse and wear a necklace. It is both far more complicated than that, and just as simple as that. Because who I am, is who I say I am.

And from that moment on, I was a girl in this young man's mind. The question had been asked and answered. That was that. No need to spend any more time trying to figure out what it all meant, or if it was right or wrong. It just was.

Stephanie Mott is a transsexual woman from Topeka, Kansas, and a nationally known speaker on transgender issues. In addition, Stephanie is the Executive Director of Kansas Statewide Transgender Education Project and a commissioner on the City of Topeka Human Relations Commission. She can be reached at stephanieequality@yahoo.com

FISHWIVES

Sally Bellerose

My wife Jackie and I teeter-totter, arm in arm, through a few inches of unshoveled snow before stepping over a dead Christmas tree to get to our car. We missed the city's curbside tree pick-up by over a month. Between us, we're 161years old, me and my Jackie. The maneuvers to get down the walk and over the tree take a few minutes.

We're both wearing puffy down parkas, the kind with fake fur around the hoods. The coats cost a fortune when they were new, got donated to the Survival Center because the fashion of encasing yourself in four bushels of airy feathers went out of style when new synthetic fibers came along. I try not to care about being out of fashion, but can't seem to stop.

When we reach the car, I flap my hand at Jackie. "You could at least drag the tree away from the curb."

Jackie winces. Her right hip still hurts from falling off a folding chair while pushing poker chips across a table. She gambles when she's depressed. Losing makes her more depressed. There's a cycle here. I give her my serves-you-right-to-suffer grin. We stand there, hanging on to the door handles, thinking our separate thoughts while we catch our breath.

I think about being old and poor. And queer. I love that the young ones have rehabilitated that word, queer. Poor, I'm afraid, is a word beyond a face lift. Poverty has always been the third woman in our marriage. We consummated our three-way lesbian alliance decades ago. We lived beyond our means and worked shitty jobs without putting a single penny toward retirement. Who knew gay marriage would become a reality? We thought the whole business of IRAs and 401Ks were a pathetic middle-class scam. Even a simple savings account was too bourgeois for us. We were too unconventional to be bothered by the unlikely fact of old age; we were radical. We flaunted being poor like it was some sexy illicit arrangement and worked nights while we got liberal arts degrees. This made Jackie a fairly well-spoken fork lift operator and me a failed novelist. We borrowed what we could and paid as little attention as possible to the bills.

But poverty is a fishwife who gets louder when ignored and meaner in old age. If it weren't for poverty shrieking "Where's the milk money?" Jackie could skim off a hundred bucks once in a while and I'd never know. For us, a hundred dollars is a week's worth of groceries, ironic, because the grocery store is where she usually gambles. Lottery tickets: a dollar, five dollars, ten dollars a pop. Hate the lottery. At least when she finds a poker game that welcomes a not-so-little old lady she exercises her mind.

People suppose your thinking slows when you're old. Sometimes my mind spins like tires stuck in a muddy field. Now, while I'm hanging on to the car's door handle, my thoughts move like an old dog circling back on its tail. I want to concentrate on a way to get her to get rid of the tree, but looking at Jackie through the little clouds my breath forms in the February air as she unlocks The Bucket, our once gold, now faded to tan, 1992 Buick, distracts me. How did Jackie get so old? The calendar, the mirror, and our joints, scream, "You're old!" I look at her all day, every day, and elderly is still a shock.

Eighty is too old to fathom. I can't even grasp that The Bucket is eighteen.

Jackie opens the door on the driver's side and says, "All the time, you're mad at me."

I ruminate on her statement. It's impossible to talk and persuade The Bucket's door to open at the same time. When we're both inside I say, "I'm only mad when you lose."

"Grilled cheese, frozen pizza, pre-washed salad in a bag with a can of tuna dumped on top." She refers to the fact that I am a lazy cook.

"Bad cook and a mediocre housekeeper, that's me. Lousy home and car repair person and mediocre luggage carrier, that's you," I say. We divided those chores fifty years ago.

We have our good points. They just haven't shown up yet today.

"I don't lose on purpose." She would sound mad to someone who doesn't know her, but I recognize her tone as regret camouflaged as irritation. At least she's talking. Yesterday she didn't say ten words.

The dead pine needles and snow stuck to my ankles make the inside of the car smell clean. I shake them off and bide my time, waiting until after Jackie buckles her seat belt and sticks the screwdriver into the hole where the car's shift should be before I continue harping on the tree. As always, she sucks in a lung full of air and sits quietly for a second after successful screwdriver insertion. When the screwdriver is in the hole, I say, "You said you'd dump the tree last weekend."

She closes her eyes as if this is going to make me, and the fishwife speaking through me, hold our tongues. When she opens them I say, "Surprise, still here."

It's after the early morning traffic and before the lunch traffic: 9 a.m. is show time for The Bucket. But even for old ladies, a few inches of fluffy snow with none in the forecast is a mild February day in New England. The suspense of whether or not the car is going to start; now that's exciting. We lean forward, exaggerating the curves of our spines. The screwdriver engages the clutch immediately and the Buick slides into first gear. We pull down the hoods of our parkas and exchange satisfied nods.

After we have a couple of miles under our wheels my head starts shaking. Jackie slows down to five miles an hour and grabs my chin with her right hand to steady my bobble-head. We've been conserving house and car fuel, haven't been for a drive in a couple of days. No wonder Jackie's been blue, with nothing to do but watch my head wobble in a cold house.

She's got that cocky look she gets when she knows she's won me over. I pull at the stubble on my face. This always gets me feeling kindly toward my wife, who calls the little plot of hair that developed on my chin my soul patch. I don't think I'll ever get over the fact that Jackie is my wife.

"It's just money," I say, tired of being stuck in the worry rut of losing the house. "You're a handsome old lady." She is: meaty, cropped grey hair, steel blue eyes with droopy lids, dignified in her butch way. I've always loved her swagger. She can't do the walk any more, but the facial expression is about the same as it was half a century ago. Butchy girls fare well, looks-wise, in old age. Compared to Jackie I'm a pretty woman, at least I've been told I'm good looking plenty of times, not recently, but in my day.

I fluff my hair. It bounces back into shape. The shape I don't mind, the white I don't mind, but the cotton candy texture, bah. I miss thick hair. I miss décolletage, my own. My cleavage was a life force, insistent, a horizontal turn on my slit of a smile. Who cares if it's more fantasy than true; I like to think I was known for my impudent slit of a smile. My smile and my décolletage were the first things Jackie noticed about me. "You have lovely teeth," she said, addressing my cleavage.

She always cracked me up, cracked me open. She infuriated me right from the start, too.

I look down at the fraying polyester quilting that covers my breasts. No wonder I live in the past. If I weed out the arguments, the money woes, the gambling, her womanizing, and my obsessive flirting, it's all me and Jackie, screwing around, having a good time. Poverty is welcome to stay the mistress in my dreams as long as my dreams stay in our past. Why not? Poor and young, I can translate in my mind, romanticize. Poor and old? Who wants to daydream about poor and old?

Jackie catches me looking in the mirror. "You're all right." She grins.

Damn if my thighs don't catch a ghost of the ache this statement used to bring on. It was the first thing she said to me at my brother's wedding in 1950. It means thank you or nice tits or I love you. I pat her leg, well below public viewing range.

Jackie squirms. To Jackie the inside of a moving car is a public place. Instead of saying she hates public shows of affection, she says, "I hate X-Mass." But she likes sacrilege. The Blessed Virgin she calls Bloodless Mary, blasphemes the entire Holy Family. Lots of names for Jesus: Stigmata Man, Parthenogenesis Boy, The Inconceivable. Joseph she calls Castrato.

Still, a few years ago she started kneeling before bed, her lips moving silently. Maybe she prays to win when she gambles. I never ask. Our days are long and the house is small. A little privacy is not too much to ask of someone who loves you.

She pulls her head back sharply, a sign that her hip is hurting.

"Tell you what," I say. "If we get rid of the tree this morning and the Social Security checks are in the mailbox when we get back, I'll buy a nice fat chicken with a dollar off coupon and roast it with those tiny red potatoes." Our company meal. When did we last have company?

She squeezes my hand, right there in the Buick, and turns around in the Langley's driveway. They moved twenty years ago, but it's still the Langley's driveway to us.

An hour later, with the help of Ramon and TJ, neighborhood boys who never seem to be in school, but always dribbling a basketball in our driveway, the tree is strapped to the roof of The Bucket. TJ slaps the hood and says, "For real, you ladies need 'a leave the handsome young TJ this car when you kick it."

"Shit." Ramon makes an ugly face at the car. "Leave me the screwdriver."

They're still grabbing their skinny sides, laughing, laughing harder because this time Jackie says "Fuck," and needs several tries before the screwdriver fits correctly in the hole.

If poverty is female, you can't prove it by the number of poor young guys in our neighborhood.

Jackie drives slowly down a dirt road to the dump. We head toward a shack with smoke curling out the chimney. I hug my handbag. Getting rid of stuff makes me optimistic. She squints and The Bucket's belly scrapes the ground as the plowed road becomes a channel of frozen tire ruts. We park next to a sign near the shack that reads, "Honk if You Need Help."

Jackie doesn't honk. She gets out of the car and limps toward the shack. My parka is blue, hers is maroon. A hairy guy, also in a parka (but his is green and grease-stained, with what might be real matted fur on the hood), comes around the tar-papered building.

He glances at the tree. "Got a sticker, buddy?"

Jackie lights up a stale cigarette without answering. She quit except for special occasions, like dumps and outside of funeral homes. She inhales, looking at him side-ways until he recognizes her and says, "Jackie? Jesus. Sorry. Been awhile."

"Thom." She nods hello. Maybe his name is Dick or Harry but it said Thom on a hat he used to wear. He was young when he wore that hat, younger than we were. Not young any more, but still younger than we are.

I get out of the car, because even though Jackie is the gambler, she won't play the poor-old-lady card. Our sticker has run out. It costs twenty-five bucks for a new one.

"Regina." He scratches his woolly beard and leans on the "Smoking Prohibited" sign.

I blush because it's come to this: A thrill that the dump guy remembers my name. "We're a little short on cash." I can't decide if I should smile, appeal to his possible love for his mother, or just look needy.

He looks around, not another soul in sight. "Five bucks. I'll help you dump it."

"We'll manage." Jackie could pass for a strong seventy when she takes her wide legged stance and looks you in the eye. "Thanks, just the same."

She pulls four singles out of her wallet. I dig in my handbag for change.

"Keep it." Thom holds up a hand. "But, I'll take a Marlboro."

"Can you believe this?" Jackie's says as Thom opens the gate to allow The Bucket entrance. She's been trying to figure an angle to roam around unescorted in this dump for years.

"He thinks we'll unload the tree and come right back like good little old ladies."

Jackie snorts. I didn't realize how worried I was about her state of mind until the relief of that snort. We drive to a fork and turn right, as Thom instructed, taking in acre after acre of his back yard. Everywhere we look—heaps of trash. I need new glasses. A thin layer of new white snow covers the dump, making things even harder to recognize, but Jackie identifies the heaps for me. "Tires. Appliances. Appliance doors. Compressed cars."

The pile of compressed cars is taller than our house. Shiny blue-black crows, smudges of black against the snow, flit from heap to heap. Seagulls squawk, a sound so prevalent it becomes background noise. I don't have to ask why Jackie stops alongside the remains of an industrial-sized freezer whose huge door has been ripped off. The view is great. From this vantage point the waste is endless, dune after dune of white blanketed stuff as far as the eye can see. Used-up stuff, huddled in the cold, tucked in for the winter.

We both get out the passenger's side, to avoid the slick road, which has been plowed but not sanded. We stand in the snow. Except for the cawing of the crows, squawking seagulls, and the occasional flapping of paper, plastic, and wings, the place is eerily quiet. The early morning sun bounces off every piece of dented chrome and broken glass that manages to stick out of the snow, even the corrugated cardboard shines.

"The Starship Enterprise crash landed on a deserted planet," she says in voice-over mode. "A world with its own rules of beauty."

I pat the sides of my parka with my puffy-gloved hands, feeling fondness for it. My feet are warm and my ankles doing fine in my quilted boots. There *is* another-worldliness here. I half expect the robots, shackled laborers, or ogres who maintain this place to appear from behind one of the trash heaps.

"THIS PLACE IS A DUMP. IF YOU WANT TO PLAY - FIND A PLAYGROUND." I read the message, painted in block letters on a piece of plywood propped next to the freezer.

"Look." Air curls out of Jackie's nostrils. She points.

I follow her gaze between the piles of rotting boards and wooden skids to a gigantic circle of... "What is that?"

"Frozen garbage. They dig a big hole, fill it with trash, and bury it. Must be too cold to work now, probably stay uncovered till spring."

I take my glasses out of my purse even though they will give me only a few seconds of improved eyesight before the heat of my breath hits the cold and crystallizes on the lenses. "A lake," I say. A frozen lake of garbage filled with the unsorted stuff of kitchen cans and dumpsters. There's a road to the lake, but it's covered with snow. "How come there's no snow on the lake?"

"Melted. Makes its own heat like a compost pile." Jackie studies the horizon like she might be asked to manage the operation some time soon. "Biggest dump in the Northeast."

"How do you know these things?" I'm always amazed at the vast difference in the facts we've accumulated in such connected lives. She shrugs. I can see by her focused squint that she plans to walk the thousand feet to get a better look.

I say, "You're an old lady with a bad hip. Snow is dangerous."

She nods as if considering the information that snow and ice are hazardous to old women with bad hips. But it's clear that she's going, and, since she's going, I'm going, too. I circle the lake with my eyes. The garbage swells in the middle. Through my foggy glasses the giant swell reminds me of an animal on its back, belly up. "The underbelly of the material afterworld, alive and exposed, vulnerable," I say.

She rolls her eyes, but smiles.

I lean my head on her shoulder and coo, "If you break your neck, I'll bitch about taking care of you 'til the day you die."

She kisses the top of my head and bends with difficulty to pick up a metal rod that looks related to the freezer. She sticks the bar in the snow. It's the perfect height for a cane, even takes a right angle at one end so she has a grip of sorts.

She offers me her arm. We plod. The few inches of snow is stabilizing, firm enough to help steady our ankles, not so deep we can't walk, fluffy enough that it might soften a fall. One step at a time, we reach a huge mustard-colored piece of equipment, a rusty bulldozer, poised near the edge of the frozen pit of rubbish.

I'm ready to sit down or lie down. Several crows flap up nervously and land again in the same spot not five feet from us.

Her cheeks are red with exertion and cold, but she looks pretty chipper. She pats the rubber tracks banding the tires of the bulldozer. "Hello, dinosaur," she says.

The big inert machine does look like a sleeping giant that probably doesn't want to be woken. The big shovel of its mouth rests on the ground and is loaded down with frozen dirt. An area in front of the machine is already covered over with earth.

"Years from now, people won't know this dump existed. It will be a retirement home for kids who are in nursery school now," she says. When we first met Jackie claimed a whole section of Boston was built on a dump. We were stoned at the time and I didn't believe her, but it turns out she was right. She looks up four tons of backhoe to stare longingly at the driver's seat, high above us inside the open cab.

"Oh no, absolutely not," I say. "Too dangerous."

"The world is full of danger. Old age. Winter." She rubs her hip distractedly. "Old and used-up are not relevant here. That's the whole point."

It's unreasonable, two elderly women standing in snow in thirty degrees, arguing about climbing into a bulldozer, but, we only made sixty years together because we're both unreasonable. This is the closest to happy Jackie's been in months. Still, it's my job to keep her from killing herself and leaving me to carry on with only one Social Security check. "Another Tonka toy you can't play with. If I could hoist you up there I would, my love."

"Shame to waste an opportunity." She steps back and considers the step up to the cab, which is at least three feet from the ground.

"The last time your foot was raised that high was in water aerobics sometime in the late nineties," I say.

She sits on the step. Then, remembering who she is, out of habit and manners, with a wince, she stands back up, offering me her seat.

"Just scoot over," I say. "We can both fit."

She struggles to sit back down, which surprises me. Down is usually easy. It's up that's the problem. I squeeze in next to her on the surprisingly generous and almost comfortable step. She leans forward with her hands on her knees, huffing. I tap my handbag, waiting for her breathing to settle down and worrying about the journey back to the car.

"Christ," she says, looking up. Her lower lip quivers. A shadow passes over us. A very large powerful looking bird, moving with slow heavy wing beats, flies by us, circling.

"Honey, it's just a hawk," I say.

She's not someone who sees omens in wildlife, still Jackie looks terrified.

"A hawk if you respect it, a buzzard if you don't," I say, trying to get her to smile, but she grabs my arm with a tenuous grip and slides off the seat to the ground in slow motion. She lands on her butt, seated in the snow.

What is happening?

"It's a bird, just a bird," I repeat, trying to convince myself that the strange look in her eye has been brought on by some sudden belief in avian angels of death. I sit next to her and pull at the back of her parka, which got bunched up when she slid off the seat of the dozer. She's too heavy to move. I give up and cradle her head between my hands.

Her face is a whole new shade of Caucasian. I pull down her hood to get a better look. Her lips are bright red against her too-white skin. Her mouth is not right. I take off my glove so I can feel her face and the pulse on her neck. I don't know what a good pulse feels like, so I settle for present.

"You're going to be okay," I say.

She gives me patronizing look. How dare she? I take off her glove, feel her clammy hand. The right side of her sagging mouth infuriates me. This is not happening. I refuse for this to be happening. A bead of sweat forms above her top lip. "Can you talk? Say something, Jackie."

She smiles at me sheepishly. "Don't be mad at me." Her voice is raspy, but otherwise deathly calm.

I pull the cell phone out of my pocket and flip it open. I've only used the thing once when I mimicked the fucking Elder Care demonstration by pretending to press the correct buttons to alert the EMS team. "Shit." My fingers are arthritic. The keyboard is small.

"A button...On the side." Jackie is paying attention.

I press every button. The screen stays black. "I've got to go get help." I pull her hood tight around her face. "Nobody dies. Not yet."

"Lucky break," she says. "Must be my heart."

"Lucky break?" Oh, she makes me angry at the worst times. I look down the road. Have we been here an hour?

"Sorry." She stops for a long moment, then looks me in the eye, all love and tenderness. "You've forgiven me." Her words are jagged, rising and falling on the wrong syllables, like the words of our friend Marvin when he was on a ventilator. "For a lot worse." She takes my hand.

I know what she wants, but it's too hard. She's not Marvin. She's my Jackie and she's staying right here with me. She'll be okay with a little cajoling, a little encouragement. "Thom will come," I say. "Just let's relax, save our energy. We can make you feel better. We can get help, there's help out there. I'm not so tired. I can do all the paperwork. I don't mind waiting in the Senior Housing Office or Elder Care. SSI, we've barely looked into SSI. And those ads on TV…" I don't know what ads I mean, but have a vague notion that I've seen ads that claim to help poor old people. And churches, churches help people. And Casa Latino, we're not Spanish, but we're in the neighborhood, they'd point us in the right direction, maybe. I'm talking a mile a minute, pulling out every social service agency and kindly friend or neighbor we've ever known.

She waits patiently, her eyes closed, whispering, "I don't crochet," when I mention The Council on Aging.

Her body is collapsing, her head into her shoulders, her shoulders into her chest. She strokes my hand weakly, comforting me, pulling her head back, using up precious energy, looking at me like there's really something to see.

"Hang on, baby. Rest. I'll get Thom. You'll go to the hospital." There are things to live for. There is me and my Jackie. "You've still got roast chicken, you still love to drive."

"Don't leave, Regina." Her words come in a loose string, unraveling. "You'll be sad about it for the rest of your life."

"Our life. And me god damn you, you've got me."

Her arm somehow is around me now. She says in a faltering pant, "We could try yoga."

I laugh, hysterical. My cackle cuts the air like an ice pick. She coughs and sputters.

I move her arm and pull her in so she's leaning on me and we can see each other's faces without much effort. "Shh, my darling," I say. She cries softly. I cry harder. We lock eyes and stop blubbering abruptly.

Her words stop. Her breathing stops. I don't breathe either, until she takes a sharp inhale. She is not dead. "Tell me a dirty story." Her words are wheezy, breathy in a bad way that scares me.

I'm disoriented, like I'm the one who's had the stroke or heart attack or whatever has happened to Jackie. She hasn't asked for a dirty story since we were in our thirties. Back then, she still had the wanderlust that made her seek out jobs hundreds, sometimes thousands, of miles away; Detroit, where she tried to get a job at GM while I stayed home in the little house on Market Street in Northampton, Massachusetts, working nights in a paper mill; Florida where she made decent money helping relocate the residents of Saint Mary's Cemetery to make room for a mall. Being us, we squandered half her paycheck on phone sex. She craved my voice giving her the audio version of sex we'd actually had. That was so sweet.

I must have said some of this out loud because she coughs out, "Sweet? No. It was good, our sex." Her chest heaves. I shush her. "Keep talking," she whispers.

But I can't. I need my wits about me to figure out how to get us out of this predicament. Old ladies don't die in dumps. Homeless men die in dumps.

She lifts her head an inch off my shoulder and says, "I'm sorry about Lorraine."

This statement orients me.

"Fuck, Lorraine," we say in unison. I pull Jackie to me. Our puffy jackets stop me from holding her as close as I want to hold her. One or both of us has said, "Fuck Lorraine," whenever one or both of us does something really stupid ever since I found out that Jackie had

had sex with another woman named Loraine in a construction site trailer in western Pennsylvania.

Jackie tries to laugh, but it pains her. I kiss her face all over. Her skin feels cold on my lips, already. No, no, I mustn't think, already. "I'll laugh for you, baby," I say stupidly, tears running down my face. She says something I almost catch. She lets her head go slack on my shoulder. I unzip the top few inches of her parka and slip my hand inside the neck of her bulky sweater. She keeps whispering, but her words are too mumbled and soft to understand. Her breast is warm. I put my ear close to her mouth.

"You're alright," she whispers and keeps whispering.

Words I understand and words I don't.

"Will we?" she says. "The newspaper?" I can't tell from her mouth if she's smiling, but her eyes seem to be laughing at the irony of her precious privacy being violated at the last possible moment.

"Oh yes, we'll make the papers, honey." I wipe drool off the side of her mouth. "I'll play your birthday in the lottery and win a lot of money." Her eyes are closed. Her mouth twitches, sounds spill out. "Shh, my love, yes, yes, you're all right." Yes, my Jackie is right, I must hold on tight and keep talking. "We're all right."

Sally Bellerose is author of The Girls Club, *Bywater Books, winner of many awards including an NEA Fellowship. Her current project* Fishwives *features old women behaving badly. The title story appears in this anthology and won first place in 2012 Saints and Sinners fiction contest. An excerpt from the novel-in-progress also appeared in BLOOM Literary Magazine. Bellerose writes about class, sex, illness, absurdity, and growing old. http://sallybellerose.word-press.com*

Fishwive*s appeared in* Saints and Sinners Fiction from the Festival 2011, *edited by Amie M. Evans and Paul J. Willis, as well as* Queer Mojo, 2011. *Fishwives also won the Saints and Sinners Short Fiction Award in 2011.*

PHYSICS FOR FIVE-YEAR-OLDS

Neil Ellis Orts

It was cold. By Houston standards, it was cold and George wore his heavier jacket as he walked down the darkening street to his friends' house. He'd just got home when Helen called, asking him to come watch Angie for a bit.

It was cold like his friend was now cold. Celeste. His college friend. She'd been sick for so long, but she always got better. It was a matter of time, of course, and this last . . . *thing*, after years of medication, treatments, near deaths and rebounds, had finally gotten her. When he saw her last, three weeks earlier, she'd said, "Prepare for the worst." He answered her, "We're never prepared for the worst."

He was right. He was not prepared for the email he got just before he left work. The email was from her brother, just the sort of guy to give bad news over email. Direct, to the point, it said, "Celeste died this morning in her sleep. Knew you'd want to know. Will be in touch with more details."

George and Celeste were the same age. Fifty. She was only 50 …

The live oaks along the street seemed to be mocking George as he walked. They were a feature he usually loved. They were, in fact, one of the reasons he decided to buy a small home down the street from Ken and Helen, but tonight their full, green foliage seemed all wrong. If your friend dies in December, there should be some stark, barren limbs reaching into the sky.

He turned up the sidewalk to Ken and Helen's house and he saw Angie through the window, sitting on the couch. At five-years-old, Angie's greetings could be unpredictable. She might run and climb up George or she might barely acknowledge his entrance. Today looked like the latter. She looked toward him, he waved, she turned her head. He could tell she was shouting into the kitchen. Helen met George at the door as he stepped onto the porch.

"Hey, George," she said. "Thank you so much for coming. I just looked online and a sweater that's perfect for Ken is on sale. They're holding one for me at Neiman Marcus."

It's perfect timing. This'll keep my mind off Celeste. I'm not ready to think about Celeste.

"Of course." George turned to Angie. "Hi, Angel Girl."

"Hi, George," Angie said. In her lap was a coloring book and in her hand was a red crayon, but her eyes were glued to the TV, where a Disney princess—one of the newer ones that George couldn't name—twirled and sang.

"I shouldn't be an hour," Helen said. "I'm just running in and out."

"You do know Christmas is next week, right?"

"Just in and out. They're holding it for me."

"I give you two hours."

She rolled her eyes. "Don't jinx me! I want to be back before Ken gets home."

"Go," George said, taking off his jacket. "The Galleria crowds are going to be thick."

Angie perked up. "What does thick mean?"

"Can you handle that?" Helen asked.

"I'm on it," George said. "Run."

"If Ken gets home before I do, cover for me."

"I'll tell him you left with a suitcase while talking to someone named Raul on your cell."

"Perfect." She turned to Angie. "Be good for George, okay sweetie?"

Then George was alone with Angie.

"George," she said in her practiced, impatient tone. "What does thick mean?" She'd recently begun asking for definitions like this, almost always for common words. Her parents had a lifestyle that gave her working definitions of phrases like "airport security," but everyday words like "thick" could puzzle her.

"Well, thick," George said, "Is the opposite of thin." He knew they did opposites in her kindergarten class. "Do you know what thin means?"

She glowered at him, another recent development. It was her latest way to tell her grownups that they weren't making sense.

"Okay," George said. "Well, here." He held up his right pinky finger. "My pinky is thin." Then he grabbed his forearm with his left hand. "And my arm is thick."

Or I could just show you a picture of Celeste in college, when she was always trying to lose weight, even though all the boys found her attractive. She was thick, but sexy. Then she got sick and thin. Let me show you a more recent picture. See? Thick. Thin.

Angie looked puzzled through her glower. "What's a thick crowd?"

"Oh, yes. I guess that's a little different. Well, a thick crowd is a lot of people. A thin crowd is fewer people. I told your mom the crowds are thick at the mall because I bet there are a lot of people there right now. It's not going to be easy for her to just run in and out."

Angie looked at her pinky doubtfully.

"Words can have more than one meaning," George said. "I guess a thick arm doesn't correlate too well to a thick crowd." George came to babysitting with a vocabulary better suited to college educated adults than kindergartners and kept talking to avoid having to define "correlate." "A thick crowd is more like a thick liquid. Do you know what a liquid is?

Glower.

"A liquid is, well, water is a liquid. You can pour it. Something that pours or spills is a liquid. Water is a thin liquid because if you spill it, it runs everywhere in no time at all. A thick liquid takes a long time to pour."

"Like what?"

George sighed. He really didn't know how to talk to children, hadn't imagined babysitting when he befriended Helen at a job, a decade earlier. She was several years younger than he, but despite her going to grad school and he moving to another job, they kept in touch. He remembered when she first started talking about Ken and how that led to marriage and eventually Angie. The unplanned evolutions of relationships can lead here, he mused. That job so many years ago lead to explaining "thick" and "liquid."

Can I tell you instead about my friend who just died? She was an elementary ed major, I was an art major, and we became inseparable from the moment she sat next to me in American history our freshman year. It was 1983 and we loved mousse, shoulder pads, and programmed drum beats. We even tried dating, before I realized I was gay. What does "gay" mean?

"Well, let's go see what's in the kitchen, huh?"

Angie slid off the couch and followed George into the kitchen. He looked around and seeing nothing on the counter, opened the refrigerator. There he saw Ken's iced tea pitcher, less than half full. In the door rack, he saw some ranch dressing. He picked up the semi-clear plastic pitcher and swirled the tea around.

"See this? How the tea sloshes around? That's a thin liquid." He returned the tea and picked up the salad dressing. He turned the bottle upside down. "See how slow the dressing runs down? That's because it's a thick liquid." He put the dressing back in the rack. "Get it?"

"I guess," Angie said.

"So imagine you had a swimming pool full of tea and another full of dressing. Tea you could swim through very easily but swimming through dressing would be very hard. The mall right now is like a swimming pool full of ranch dressing."

"You're crazy, George."

"I know, sweetie." George closed the refrigerator and saw the ice maker on the door. "Oh, and here is some really thick liquid. It's so thick it's solid!"

"What are you talking about, George?"

"Ice is water. You knew that, right?"

Angie rolled her eyes. "Yes." Ken and Helen had been trying to break Angie of her new habit of rolling her eyes, but George couldn't bring himself to say anything, especially since it copied Helen so perfectly.

"Well then, do you know what steam is?"

"That's what comes off hot food. Then you have to blow on it."

"That's right," George said. "Steam is pretty much very hot water in its vapor form, rising off the food."

Glower.

"I guess you haven't had a physical science class yet, huh?"

Glower.

"Well, let's do something really simple and you'll have something to tell your teacher about after Christmas."

George reached into the cabinet where his friends kept their cooking pots and pulled out a sauce pan. He held it under the ice maker and a few ice cubes like rocking chair runners clattered into the pan.

"Okay, watch this." George pulled a chair from the breakfast nook over to the stove and lifted Angie to stand on it. "Water—well, lots of things—has three physical states. Ice is the solid state of water. The water we drink is the liquid state, and steam is what we call the gaseous or vapor state."

"What are you talking about, George?"

I'm not talking about my dead friend, Celeste. I'm talking about elementary physical science to a five-year-old because I'm not talking about my dead friend, Celeste.

"Just watch. What do you think will happen to the ice cubes when I turn on the heat?"

Angie rolled her eyes. "They'll melt."

"That's right. See? It's happening already."

The ice cubes began to slide in the puddles they were creating and soon, they were slivers floating in rapidly heating water.

See that? How skinny the ice is getting? That's how Celeste melted away. That's exactly how her arms melted down to bony slivers.

"So see? It was a solid and now it's almost all liquid."

Angie was quiet as she watched the last slivers disappear in the water. George smiled. He was glad to know that some simple things could still hold her attention enough for her to drop her kindergartner cool.

"Do you know what it means for water to boil?"

"It's how you make spaghetti!" she said.

"Well, yes, that's the first step for making spaghetti," George said. "But we're not making spaghetti now. See in the bottom of the pan, the bubbles there?"

"Yeah."

"Those are little pockets of steam forming. The heat is turning the water into steam, the vapor state of water."

Angie watched, entranced, as the bubbles formed and rose to break the water's surface.

And that? That steam is like my friend's breath, escaping into the air. She's vapor now, boiled away by that damned virus. She boiled away in fever sweats and diarrhea, until there was only the residue of a few friends left behind. Friends like this one gay man who somehow escaped the virus, despite being no safer than she was 25 years ago. She is now vapor and I am solid but wanting to melt away.

"George, are you crying?"

"Oh no, Angel Girl." He wiped his eyes. "I got some steam in my eyes and it burned a little."

It's a weak lie, Angel Girl, but it's the type of thing grown-ups say to a five-year-old. It's easier, like the way physics is easier to explain than grief.

"Let's go play dolls," Angie said and hopped off the chair. The physics lesson was over.

"Okay, Angel Girl." George turned off the burner and followed her into her bedroom. They set up Barbie table and chairs with skinny dolls, most of them princesses and princes that he didn't recognize. Angie supplied most of the dialog for the dinner party. He just had to hold one or two up to the table.

An old friend died today, Angel Girl. She would be amused to see me sitting on a floor with you, playing dolls. She would be appalled that I didn't tell you about condensation, how vapor will return to water. Celeste taught elementary school science before she went on disability. She wouldn't have left out that part. Death and birth and death and birth. That's from a Joni Mitchell song, I forget which one. Not one of her better-known ones. Death and birth and death and birth. Celeste would know it.

"Hey, listen," George said, hearing a door open. "I bet that's your mom back already." He grunted as he got up.

"We're not finished!"

"C'mon! Let's go see what she bought."

Glower.

It wasn't Helen, but Ken.

"Oh hey, George."

Angie shuffled down the hallway behind George.

"Hey, Angie," Ken said and scooped her up in his arms, kissing her cheek. "What have you been up to?"

"Playing dolls with George."

Ken smiled at George. "Good times, huh? Is Helen home?"

"No she asked me to watch Angie for a bit. She had an errand to run."

"Where'd she go?"

67

George hesitated. "I'm not sure, but she went to the car talking on her cell to someone named Raul."

Ken chuckled and set Angie down again. "Oh my wife and her Latin lovers."

"Don't tell her I told you. I think it's supposed to be a secret."

"Right. Well, I've noticed she seems to take up with them right before Christmas. You staying for dinner? I don't know what we're having, but you're welcome."

"No thanks, not tonight." George picked up his coat and put it on. "I had some bad news today. A college friend just died …"

"I'm sorry, George. Someone close?"

"I've talked about her to you and Helen. Celeste."

"I remember. Anything you need?"

George gave his head small quick shakes. "I just want to make a couple of phone calls, make sure other people in our circle know. That sort of thing."

"You sure you don't want to stay for dinner first?"

"I'm not very good company right now." George smiled and nodded towards Angie, who'd gone back to her room. "Ask her—I was giving her physics lessons, all about solids, liquids, and vapors."

"Sounds heavy," Ken said.

"It seemed appropriate in the moment. Easier, anyway, than explaining death."

"No doubt." George opened the front door and Ken continued, "Come back if you change your mind."

"Thanks."

Outside, it had gotten colder. As he walked, George pulled out his cell and called Helen, told her that Ken was home, and that she could drop off his present at his place if she wanted. She said she might, that she was still stuck in horrendous traffic by the Galleria. He said, "I told you so," and he could almost hear her eyes rolling.

They hung up. He looked to the sky, thin clouds illuminated from below by the light pollution of Houston. Vaporous clouds. *Death and birth and death and birth.* He wondered if it would freeze overnight. He thought it might.

Neil Ellis Orts is a writer and performer, whose work has appeared in Blue Rock Review, The Dying Goose, *and* Saint Katherine Review, *as well writing the occasional article on arts or religion for local media. His novella,* Cary and John, *was published in 2014. He produces performance work under Breath & Bone/Orts Performance and is usually very tired because he does all this around a full-time day job. He searches Amazon with keywords like "theological aesthetics." Unsurprisingly, he lives alone with a cat in Houston, Texas.*

BATTERY CITY

Dominic Ambrose

It was Reneya, I reminded myself, like the name René with a "Ya!" on the end. The subtle change that Reneya's name had taken over the years seemed to be of considerable importance to her, so I reminded myself to go along. Then I dove back in and listened as Reneya went on and on. Reneya was still talking about those two people, her friend Delphina and Delphina's beau, whom she kept calling Krauthammer, like I knew them. Now, Reneya has been an incorrigible dirty talker since the day I met her, soooo many years ago as a teenager, so I wasn't too surprised when her chatter began taking on the forms of foreplay as we headed over to meet the male half of the couple. She had worked herself up to a frenzy by the time we approached the entrance to the promenade bar in Battery Park City.

Reneya's foreplay:

"Now, let me see, what was it that Delphina said to Krauthammer? He's a philosopher, you know, besides being a scientist. So she says, 'Explain Aristotle to me.' Yeah right, Aristotle. And Galileo and Copernicus too, I suppose. The guy took it in his stride explaining away like she was really listening, as she sipped her drink. I know her, I know what was going on in Delphina's dirty mind. She was undressing that little East German with her eyes, and whatever her bloodshot eyes couldn't focus on, she invented. I'm sure every time he shifted his weight she looked down to get a glimpse of the bulge in his pants. Am I being too gross? Sooorryyy. I could just hear her, when he was talking about the earth circling the sun she was imagining his wet tongue circling her labia majoris, yeah, that's right, Krauthammer, just keep on circling that hot sun."

"... Oh, she didn't say that, did she?" I said, doubtful that this Delphina person could talk half as dirty as my Reneya.

"No but that was definitely what she was thinking or maybe it's just my own dirty mind you know me too well," she said without punctuation, then paused to get another wind and a bit of inspiration. "But she did tell me later that she was going to douche the Sigmund Freud right out of her vagina and make room for Krauthammer."

I mentally rolled my eyes. Knowing Reneya, I doubted that Delphina said anything of the sort. Krauthammer! Is that really his name?

"No, I just call him that for fun. It's really Heinz, or Franken or Stein."

Her voice tripped on the last one. Stein was her own last name, her real one, before she changed it to Bliss. Reneya Bliss. I didn't say anything but she knew I knew. We'd been friends from high school, when this dirty talk began, and apparently never stopped.

We got to the bar, and there he was. A bouncy little guy around fifty, and thus a full decade younger than us. He was overweight and balding and decidedly unpleasant looking. He jumped down from the stool and gushed excitedly as Reneya approached. "Oh, ma belle! Quelle surpreeeezuh!"

Yeah, what a surprise, indeed.... wasn't this meeting at his own insistence? I wondered why he was called Krauthammer. I looked down at his fly and didn't see the tracings of anything prodigious lurking there. Maybe it was because he was built like a solid sack of vegetables? Or a stalk of Chinese cabbage rotting in the sun? He wore an old, off-the-rack business suit, the way men wore business suits at all hours of the day and night back before our time. His looked like it hadn't been cleaned or pressed since the turn of the century. The turn of *which* century was yet to be determined.

He fumbled and kissed her hand drunkenly. Reneya told him she was just enjoying the beautiful autumn day, with an old friend from "her youth." He ignored me and said that she must have looked formidable (for-mee-DAH-bluh!) in the glistening afternoon sun. Yes, she admitted, because she was showing her old friend around her neighborhood. "Oh really?" he gazed around at his unattended drink.

"Yes." I said simply trying to reel the little twerp in.

"This is my old friend, Dominic."

"Oh, Doh-mineeek!" he gushed again as he turned to me. "I am Herr Doktor Gunther Heinz Hausbrenner! Enchanté! Are you from France?"

"No, I am from here. Pleased to meet you," I replied.

Ah, the pleasure was all mine, until I just spit it right back out, like the bartender just served me a glass of piss on the rocks!

Well, no, he didn't really say that. Now I'm getting as bad as Reneya. But for sure that is what he could have been saying, such was his body language and the expression on his face as the smile immediately dropped away and the disgust set in when I spoke. Jeesh, was it my New York accent? ... not nearly as posh as the phony trash that Reneya was peddling. Or maybe my high voice, nothing the least bit alpha male about that. Or maybe I just had bad breath. In any case, he quickly shifted around to face Reneya and put his disappointment in me on the back burner for the rest of their conversation.

I must have missed some bon mot, because Reneya was already midsentence in conversation when I came back from my reverie.

"Oh, right!" Reneya was laughing. "I know all about that. They almost threw you in jail in East Germany for that protest! You're so brave! Lavinia told me all about it."

Krauthammer or Herr Doktor Hausbrenner or whatever took Reneya's hand and pulled it close to him just as he awkwardly regained his perch on the barstool, in the process bringing her French tipped fingernails dangerously close to his threadbare crotch.

"Really, you know about me, my darling?" he gurgled.

"Oh yes, all kinds of things," Reneya babbled.

"So tell me what you know about me. Is it really something or are you just saying?" (laugh laugh).

"Oh, yeah," she assured with ostentatious mendacity. "You know girls talk. Take the measure of things, that sort of thing." She withdrew her French tipped fingers from the environs of his nether area.

He didn't catch the innuendo. "Tell me Reneya!" He demanded. He was drunk and pretty thick and so enamored with his own line that he kept hammering away at it, so to speak, without bothering to hear the answer.

She just laughed.

"What do you know about me? Reneya!" He again grabbed her right hand and stroked it.

She took up her drink with her left, and sipped it.

"Re- Nay- Ahhhhh!" *(The little sack of onions was getting too loud.)* "What a name! It is exotic! Something mysterious! Latin, Italian or something!"

"Or something." she agreed.

Actually, it was Jewish from East New York. Her father had a clothing store on Pitkin Avenue and a cart at the street market on Sundays. Remember, I knew her from high school. She had been René in high school, but had insisted on being called Rene-uh, even by the teachers, who occasionally obliged. She told her friends it was her nickname, which was odd, since a nickname was supposed to be shorter, not longer, we were all totally sure. Eventually, it became general knowledge that she was Rene-uh because her mother had not been content to have her daughter called by the simple foreign name René, elegant but rather undernourished, so with her babuschka accent, she had added another syllable at the end, for good measure. Rene-uh, such a little bubala! But good lord, what was I thinking. Time to pull myself back in to the lah and the dee and the dah of this conversation. Hausbrenner took a breather from his hammy performance in order to guzzle the rest of his drink. Then he looked at me significantly as he danced the now empty glass in his upraised hand.

I ignored the opportunity to become his liquid benefactor and instead gave Reneya a tortured look of my own. "We have a few more stops to make," I reminded her, and she immediately slithered out of Herr Doktor's grip and we bid that drunken Houseburner adieu.

"He's a horny little fuck," I said once we were back on the street.

"Yes," she laughed, giving every indication that she had thoroughly enjoyed the meeting with Hausbrenner AKA Krauthammer. Although it had been painfully obvious that Hausbrenner had spent the entire encounter putting the make on Reneya, she didn't seem to care about the irony of it. It had been just another opportunity to chatter away this lazy autumn afternoon. In fact, when Reneya went back to her famous storytelling, it was all about Lavinia and her true love. Lavinia was so in love with him. Head over heels in love with this little East German.

"She was devastated when he didn't win the Nobel Prize," Reneya said, almost in a trance, as though she were channeling Jacqueline Susann as she penned *Valley of the Dolls*. "They announced the winners last week, with no mention of the famous Dr. Krauthammer!"

"Herr Doktor Hausbrenner." I corrected. This was getting too confusing.

"Hausbrenner," she conceded. "Lavinia wouldn't talk to any of us for days. They met a month ago on the tenth anniversary of 9/11. Krauthammer, or Dr. Hausbrenner, as I should really call him, was sitting on a bench by the river and he asked her in Spanish if he could buy a cigarette from her. She said he could have one, she had answered Sí! She was proud of her Spanish. She always goes to those places on vacation, you know, so she added the word, Gratis! to indicate that she did not require payment."

(cobbling together an efficient, if somewhat artless utterance, I mused.)

"So he asked if she was more comfortable in English. 'It is amazing how many people speak Spanish in this city,' he had said."

(and judging from the photo that Reneya had shown me, it would indeed have been amazing if this blonde and blue eyed Lavinia were one of them.)

"And he said, 'It's Spanish just like what you hear in Cuba. I studied there, you know.'"

"Oh, how interesting," she must have said, I wasn't there but she must have said.

"They do their best, with what they've got," he must have said with a shrug.

(conceding this magnanimously, and thus shifting his impressiveness to how quickly he could dismiss the Cuban university system.)

He took her to breakfast, then to lunch, then to dinner. The next morning he went back to Boston where he was lecturing at BU, but he couldn't stay, he couldn't get that harbor siren out of his mind.

"He took the morning bus back to New York to stay with Lavinia. They went out to bars and clubs all night. At one bar we were all there sitting with the Italian couple, they live over there in that building behind mine, you see it? And we were sitting there in this crowded bar on Broadway, very elegant, and this lady passes by wearing this lacy bra with cutouts for her nipples. And when she squeezes past Lavinia, she must have squeezed pretty damn close because her nipple gets caught on one of Lavinia's fine gold neck chains. She wears these super long, fine chains like a garland? They get caught on everything. So Lavinia jumps up like I have never seen her jump before and she trails up after the bra woman, like she's about to kiss her butt. She's saying Stop!, Stop!, and the woman turns around and looks at her, then turns back away like Lavinia is just another local crazy, and Lavinia's still calling Stop! and the woman finally stops and listens. 'Your knob! My chain is caught on your knob!' 'My what? Oh'."

I tried to picture the scene. Is that even possible? I thought maybe Reneya was getting carried away a bit. I thought maybe we should carry ourselves away somewhere else.

"Let's go to Occupy Wall Street!" I suggested.

So we went to Zuccotti Park. It was a grungy mess—sleeping bags, garbage, recycling, pots, pans and Tupperware, and used books for sale or gift. Lots of paper items. Besides the books there were leaflets, and small signs to label all kinds of things, even labeling the people artfully snuggled on the concrete who did not want their pictures taken. "No photos!" the sign said, and I regretfully put my camera halfway into my pocket as I passed them. Most of all, there were soggy piles of political signs made of cardboard.

SIGNS:
More Green No More War
Free Energy
Tax the Rich
Imprison Wall Street
and the ubiquitous "We Are the 99 Percent!"

The park was a barrage of wordy slogans, musings, and other earnest talk. Never before had I seen such an articulate and verbose encampment of homelessness. There were long-worded posters propped up against the fences explaining every illegal economic phenomenon, from Ponzi schemes to Savings and Loan fraud to Collusion, Cartel and Monopoly. This was a Hooverville with a college degree. There was a man playing a large red conga drum and further along, an elderly man with long, fluffy, blond-grey hair strumming a guitar. There was a black man in sandals and pajama-striped pants on a ledge lecturing about imperialism and another in multi-colored stretch pants and roller blades holding up a Styrofoam peace sign with the legend, "Shitcan Teaparty - America's Douchebags!" A young woman seated on the ground was selling wobbly canvases of bad art and an elderly lady with short snow-white hair moved as though sailing along the narrow lanes between the detritus. This last one was immediately noteworthy.

"She looks like an original—from the sixties!" Reneya said with surreptitious enthusiasm. The woman was indeed surreal in her striking gold lamé trench coat. She moved as though through a film that Fellini would have shot if he had been a New Yorker. She smiled distantly at the hippies squatted out below as she strode amidst her entourage, a group of four or five men a good deal shorter than her, and dressed down in jeans and open-collar shirts.

"Her coat is pure Carnaby Street," Reneya said.

"Goldfingah!" I sang, like Shirley Bassey. "I used to love that song."

"I did, too," Reneya said. "Goldfinger!," she repeated with Bassey's intonation.

Someone said, "Megaphone!" in this loud, portentous voice. He said it just once, but that was enough for several people throughout the park to respond in raggedy unison, "Megaphone!" just as momentously.

Then there was a sudden lull in the hubbub.

"The cops are arresting people on the Brooklyn Bridge!"

"The cops are arresting people on the Brooklyn Bridge!" a much larger group of bystanders repeated loud, but in more perfect union.

"They have called upon us here in the park to join them!"

"They have called upon us here in the park to join them."

The call from the megaphone guy and imitative response from the crowd reminded me of the bored unison mumblings of Sunday mass, the congregation stumbling through their early morning mea culpas just barely bothering to understand the words that are coming out of their own mouths. Now I was really in uncharted territory. Was this the labor solidarity of yore, in militant twenty-first century style, or was this the set of a movie about totalitarian nightmares?

"The NYPD has declared open season on Occupy Wall Street!"
"The NYPD had declared open season on Occupy Wall Street!"
"So now all of us who can, are going to join them!"

...

But then the chorus did not respond immediately, and the spell was broken.

"Why?" another voice said nearby.

The megaphone person shrugged his shoulders. "It was decided at the meeting. Maybe you agree, maybe you don't."

That led to more deliberations and more commentary until the hubbub had been fully restored.

A few minutes later we saw the Goldfinger lady being interviewed for the New York One cameras. She was looking steadfast into the camera and articulating something rather longwinded into the mike as we approached. Her important looking entourage formed a semi-circle backdrop for the camera.

"It's like deja vu all over again," I said.

"I love it," Reneya replied. "I did this! I did this years ago! Forty years ago!"

"So did I." I lamely elbowed my way into the limelight. "But it does seem different now."

Two white girls who looked not yet twenty were conspicuous in their miniskirts and revealing tops. They stood vaguely facing each other, shifting their weight from one skinny bare leg to the other. They held up signs, one of which said *Wall Street, eat my twat!* The other said *Bankers: quit jerking us off!* and featured a crude dick and balls illustration just to underscore the point. I stared at them, their lipstick, their miniskirts practically up to their crotches, wondering what their game was. Then I noticed a man like a plainclothes detective standing another distance away, watching me watching them. He smirked and gave me a wink.

"Oh, fuck!" Reneya said as she stepped in something gooey.

I tried another truism on for size. "The more things change the more they stay the same."

"Been here, done this," Reneya said as she inspected her shoe. "Now, let's get lost."

Back at Reneya's apartment. Reneya stuffed a corncob pipe with tobacco from a little brass Buddha that opened at the belly as I watched the evening take hold over New Jersey and the harbor islands. The Statue of Liberty was right outside of her freaking window!

"I work for Macho Mayonnaise," she said loudly, snapping me back to this world. "It's just me and Lonnie. No, it's not really mayonnaise! That's just the name. Where have you been? It's lube. I don't have any personal expertise in this stuff at all, but as I understand it, when one of you guys has this big, meaty thing and you are trying to stuff it into one of those tight little bungholes, where it wasn't supposed to go in the first place, you need some help, some lubricating help."

"Oh, anal lubricant," I said, "Sorry, Reneya, I am so out I am waiting for that to be in."

"Well, then maybe you should use some Macho Mayonnaise. Goes in like a dream. It's a wonderful product. I hope you guys appreciate it, it's whipped with a mother's loving care, even if the package has this bimbo Marlboro man doing the whipping."

"I am sure they do appreciate it, Reneya. What could be a greater honor for a cream than to be smeared all over a juicy erect dick," I asked her rhetorically, as I didn't think she would have an answer. She had none, so I continued. "...as it glides snugly into that hole it was most definitely made for!"

But now she was thinking about Lonnie.

"He is wonderful, I love him like a son. And very unusual. He is tall, six feet and more and that is strange because he is Israeli and you don't expect Israelis to be tall. He's hairy and dark, like an Israeli, though, but not fat, he works out like a hamster. What do you call them when they're hairy like that and thin, like a bear but not? A Teddy? A cub? It's like a running joke with us because his partner is Harold, and he once showed me an old picture of himself as a Cub Scout. So after that in my mind they're the Two Cubbies. I call them that and they laugh. Lonnie just has this one product and the company was floundering. I got it back on its feet and now we are making a profit. Oh, you like those lamps, you see? They're all over the place, there, there and there. I made them myself. This one is all green marbles. That one I found all those banana shaped glass pieces."

"Do you sell them?"

"No, not yet. They're not perfect yet."

The eighteen-year-old cat got up on the coffee table and started to sniff around the apple pastry that sat hardening there.

"Get away from there!" Reneya said, but the cat ignored her. Then she picked the cat up and deposited her with a throw somewhere a bit distant. A thump was heard as her paws hit the carpet. "She knows it's her house," Reneya explained.

"I'm eighteen years old and I'll do whatever the hell I want" I said, doing my best impression of the feline queen, at the same time getting a mental image of Reneya herself at eighteen years old, who would have been perfectly capable of making that statement—at least once daily. A long life had gone by since then, as Reneya had told me, a life full of joys and disappointments, a man loved and lost, a flood-destroyed house in New Jersey, a son with legal issues, an older brother who no longer spoke to her after the death of his own son. And with all that, Reneya was still here, still unique and adventurous and bold as ever. I realized how little the superficial things mattered here, because she didn't live in that superficial world, just skated through it, like the lady in gold lamé. She lived somewhere else, somewhere within, somewhere pure where she could burn bright underneath it all. I admired her for that and I basked in the warm glow.

"That's right, it's her house and she can do what she wants!" Reneya said, as she gazed at the cat, now engaged in sweet misbehavior elsewhere in the room. "And you know what? She's right. I probably would have let her stay there nibbling if you weren't here. She's just like me, so we understand each other perfectly."

Dominic Ambrose is the author of two gay-themed novels, Nickel Fare, *set in Brooklyn in the 1970s, and* The Shriek and the Rattle of Trains, *set in Romania in the 1990s. He is a native New Yorker, inspired in equal parts by his travels to other places and by his own ever changing hometown. Presently, he lives on Staten Island, just above the harbor, where he dedicates his time to his writing and his photography. His latest projects are a photographic book about Uzbekistan and a memoir collaboration with Rain, a stylist/practitioner who assists clients with their trans-transformations. Memoirs are a special preoccupation for him, as he prepares his own real stories for eventual publication. Although this is a work of fiction, "Battery City" is an example of the short portraits and scenarios that will someday become an autobiographical collection.*

AT FIFTY

Allison Green

We have entered the last half of our lives. Our friends are old enough to die of old diseases. We grew up with little knowledge of death. Our mother died young. Our first lover died of epilepsy. The only ones we knew who died were relatives in dark, curtain-drawn places with pretty teacups we weren't allowed to touch and plates of cookies we weren't allowed to plunder. There was a boy in high school who died drag-racing, but we had to look him up in the yearbook to see who he was.

We spent our youth trying things on. We were singers in the high school musical, poets in cafes, street musicians on the Ave. We were girlfriends, best friends, spurned friends, untrusted, and trustworthy friends. We feathered, shagged, and wedged our hair. We drew green eye shadow above our eyebrows, wore bubble-gum flavored lip gloss, refused to wear lipstick, wore too much lipstick. We wore togas to Latin club, memorized lines, mostly won at chess. We marched against the draft. We had sex, didn't have sex, had everything but sex. We went to our first concert; it was at the Kingdome with 16,000 people. We went to an all-ages disco. We were asked to sit down after dancing with a girl. This isn't that kind of place, they said.

We went off to college in places like Olympia, Eugene, Berkeley, Northampton. We fact-checked for the *Atlantic*, took dictation, talked phone sex in a Manhattan basement, drove a taxi, kept on playing our music, writing our poems, taking our photographs. We marched for women's rights and gay rights. We marched against the invasion of Grenada. We smoked pot, dropped acid, took mushrooms, went sober. We drank wine out of Dixie cups.

Our cats traveled the country with us. We sailed halfway around the world with a family friend. We packed our bags for graduate school on the other coast. We drove from Boston to Seattle, sleeping in dark, empty campgrounds in the open air. We stopped at the Corn Palace. We sent postcards. We sent long, juicy letters. We called, out of the blue, on our birthdays and got drunk over the phone.

We fell in love. We had boyfriends who wrote us songs and built giant puppets, girlfriends who took our portraits. We made domestic nests of candles and ferns. We slept with other people and confessed. We slept with other people and didn't confess. We lusted only in our hearts. We stayed loyal for years and years and years until someone new cracked our hearts open and we realized we'd been unhappy. We spent years alone and decided we liked it. We fell hard, very hard, and then he said he wasn't ready for marriage, but within a year he was married to someone else. We went to couples counseling. It helped a lot. We broke up anyway. We went to individual counseling. It helped a lot. With the next lover, we knew what we wanted.

We had abortions, we had babies, we stopped having sex with men and didn't worry about babies. Some of us had weddings. Some would wait years for weddings. Some couldn't give a shit about weddings. We tried to adopt but it didn't work out. We inseminated for a year, but it didn't take. We got pregnant before we were ready but what the hell; we had a beautiful, beautiful baby. We fell in love with our nieces and nephews and friends' children. They rode on our backs and climbed in our laps and fell asleep in our arms. Our ability to embrace these new responsibilities surprised the hell out of us.

We went to medical school. We earned master's degrees in fine arts, library science, literature. We didn't go to graduate school because we kept getting promoted. We learned to bind books. We made millions at a new company on the eastside that did something with computers. We were awarded a prize for our first published short story. We gave readings, we gave talks, we interviewed for new jobs. We taught, edited, wrote, photographed, supervised, healed, catalogued. We discovered we had a talent for teaching yoga.

We came home. We never left home. We couldn't stay away from the Cascades and the Olympics, glittery on the horizon. We missed water. We missed, specifically, Puget Sound. We missed inlets and rocky beaches and blue herons. We missed ferries and the keening gulls that follow them. We missed coffee culture. We came home, but we put the entire city between us and our parents. We came home, but we put three hours between us and our parents. We moved back into our parents' neighborhood, having forgiven them and having been forgiven.

We have entered the last half of our lives. We get small parts in plays at Seattle Rep. We publish essays in obscure journals. We play with Instagram. We teach, edit, write, photograph, supervise, heal, catalog. We drink wine from fancy glasses. We never even think about drinking anymore. We have weaned ourselves of trans fats, salt, and gluten. We love cupcakes and truffle fries. Our children are going to college now. Our favorite dogs, long gone, run in photographs on our desks. Our parents are more frail. Our parents just walked the Camino in Spain. Our parents are gone. We have lost some friends to cancer. We want, most of all, time alone to work and think and breathe. We want, most of all, to laugh with friends in candlelight and communion. We want, most of all, to make sure our loved ones know we love them, to know our loved ones love us. We want, most of all, to be. At least a few more years.

Allison Green is the author of a novel, Half-Moon Scar *(St. Martin's), and a memoir forthcoming from Ooligan Press. Her work has appeared in* Zyzzyva, Calyx, Bellingham Review, Defunct, *and other publications. She lives and teaches writing in Seattle.*

LIFE SHRINKAGE

James P. Reynolds

I.

"We are twins," Thelonious would often say. He and Dave shared the same birthday; the same birth year. "We understand each other."

Thelonious went over to the stereo and put on the old CD of Monk tunes that he had brought over, tunes played by his favorite defunct Swedish piano trio – the Esbjorn Svensson Trio. This was not normally Dave's first choice, but darned if he didn't have these occasional cravings for it that were so like food cravings that, when he listened to this trio's youthful pianist interpreting his band's selection of Monk's timeless songs, he was never surprised to find himself pining for the days when he could eat anything he wanted.

He was not well enough to think about food today, however. It never made him feel any better either, remembering how Esbjorn had perished in a diving accident, lost and alone at the bottom of the sea.

Thelonious, a person with a developmental disability, Oscar's ex-patient from his community nursing days, went and sat back down. He had slowly become one of Dave's closest friends. He was, by far, the most interesting person in their desperate and shrunken lives—Oscar's and Dave's desperately shrinking lives.

Oscar had to put off early retirement, mainly to keep up the long-term health benefits for Dave.

Sometimes on these visits, Thelonious would tell Dave disturbing bedside stories about his years in the institution; all the more disturbing because Thelonious had a sense of humor about it, and it was literally impossible not to laugh until you cried. Dave inevitably needed more drugs to get to sleep those nights, but he would never think of asking Thelonious to stop telling his Woodlands Asylum stories. Lest we forget…

Thelonious still has the same partner from his institutional days. Johnny. He married Johnny in an intimate dual ceremony with Oscar and Dave as soon as gay marriage was legal, back in 2005, but Thelonious and Johnny have been together, against all odds, since the '70s.

Thelonious rarely brings the middle-aged but nonetheless hyperactive Johnny with him for these contemplative jazz visits, though.

Dave looked down from the heights of his home hospital bed. Whenever Oscar was at work, Thelonious whiled away hours at a time sitting there in the lounge chair beside him, telling him (usually uplifting) stories, or reading to him, or just sitting quietly.

Thelonious was truly psychic when it came to understanding Dave's now solely non-verbal communication.

But the jazz was playing, and Thelonious, as always when the jazz was playing, but especially when it was the music of his immortal namesake, held on to Dave's shaking, skeletal hand, and with his eyes closed, rocked his graying head silently in perfect synch with the impossible time signatures.

II.

Thelonious was at the door, but by the time Oscar answered, he had turned away to watch his bus silently move off into the traffic. When Thelonious turned back around to the view through the open door into the living room, he was still moved by the sight of the returned sofa; the missing bed.

Every time he had come to visit Oscar over the last few months, Thelonious tried sitting on the sofa, but every time the spirit of the bed – of Dave's bed – seemed to rise up and pressurize him. The pressure caused tears to flow; quiet, draining tears. Sadness and depression, Thelonious felt quite sure, are as much a physical, external pressure as anything psychological.

Regardless, he went straight to the couch again this time. He *wanted* to feel comfortable there. But while Oscar was busy in the kitchen, Thelonious wiped his eyes and moved over to his lounge chair.

Oscar returned with two glasses of beer. They had taken to sharing a beer or two on these recent visits.

No music, no disruptive Johnny, not much discussion, just two friends quietly enjoying a few sips of beer together and deeply missing their dear departed soul-mate.

James P. Reynolds has been writing fiction for many years, but only recently started sharing it with the outside world. James lives with his partner in Vancouver, British Columbia, and hosts a popular book collecting website featuring essays about his own collection of modern literary fiction. For 25 years, he has worked to promote equality for people with intellectual disabilities. He currently manages Spectrum Press, producing educational materials by, for, and about people with disabilities. He has written two works of disability rights literature.

JUST BE GLAD YOU HAVE HEELS

Jane Eaton Hamilton

A girl on the ferry—17? 18?—leans over and tells you her sister was born without calcaneums, the bones in the feet that form the heels. She goes on to outline operations and medical procedures involving surgeries and physical therapies so grim they make the butterfly bandages on your chest curl. You say life is tough. Why, even for you. You tell her that three weeks ago you had a mastectomy for breast cancer. The girl frowns hard. She cuts a look at you. She says, "Oh, for pity's sake. You must be what? 30 years old? 35? Old? You've had your life. And honestly, you ought to just be glad you have heels."

Heels? You look down at the general vicinity of your heels wishing you were glad to have them.

You're not glad, either, for being underemployed. Or happy your house has a leaking roof and a flooding basement. Or pleased about the chemotherapy which will pitch you into menopause even though you and Claire have been trying to conceive. You even grouse about the single thick hair that sprouts, blackly, from your undiseased breast like a miniature flagpole. It seems to you that if you had to have a breast removed, it could have been that one. Maybe at Pride this year you will go topless, attaching a tiny rainbow flag to the hair's tip.

You could be dying, is the thing. Why would you care about heels?

The House of a Thousand Flowers, your B+B, clings desperately to the eroding cliffs of the Ucluelet shoreline. When the owner greets you, shambling out from under a stick-laden pergola, a scruffy elderly Lab retriever hops on three legs to his side. The owner wears only shorts and taupe vinyl sandals. Sleet cuts sideways though the air flattening his chest-hairs. You yourselves are dressed in camouflage gear and bulky fleeces.

"Call me Skip," the man says and grabs your hand between two beefy ones. Plump, he has a fizz of pure white hair, a bulbous nose with exploded capillaries, and bowed legs covered with angry red scabs. His ankles are bigger than his calves.

Claire shuffles bags—she's carrying her own and yours, because you can't—and vigorously shakes his hand. Because she has a fondness for things horticultural, she says, "Are you the gardener?"

"Oh, we do try," Skip says. Ice crystals melt on his lashes. He bends down and ruffles the scabrous dog's neck. "We love our wisteria, don't we, snookums? In another month or two, the most darling racemes will positively drip from these vines." He points up. His nails, nearly an inch long, are perfectly buffed.

There isn't a flower in sight.

Indoors is as revoltingly green as outdoors was disappointingly brown. House of a Thousand Misleading Advertisements. Skip leads you over shag rugs that haven't been raked in decades. You descend a staircase with a rickety cast iron banister, down to a basement room, his sandals snapping against his heels (is he grateful for his heels? *Is* he?). The dog's nails click on the linoleum.

"Ah," Claire says when Skip opens the bedroom door.

It is difficult to speak. The room is painted a bilious aqua. There is a double bed with a slippery Wal-Mart bedspread, thin strips of unframed but beveled and etched mirror plastered to one wall, a latticey orange swag lamp. Nowhere to sit except one lawn chair with frayed and hanging strapping.

Just be glad you have a butt.

"Oh," you say.

"We call this scrumptious palace the Tea Room," Skip says. "For you ladies, our premiere accommodations."

At least the view of islands and pounding surf is breathtaking. You can see whales, faint hurricane shaped blows, far off near the horizon. Hummingbirds, unfazed by the unfurling end of winter, their throats startling and iridescent, dive-bomb red sugar water in a feeder, buzz like overgrown bees. Skip leads you around the corner to a hot tub. Algae covered, filthy, it steams under a sway-backed shack.

Your absent breast itches unmercifully. You lie down gingerly, worried about bugs, filth and infection. You wanted this weekend to be special. Claire has spent two months indulging you, and more months are on their way, the months of chemotherapy. You wanted to pamper her a little. You wanted to spoil her. You cant yourself up on one elbow. "Does it stink in here or is it just my imagination?"

You sniff as she sits beside you.

"House of a Thousand Promising Brown Sticks," she says. "Are you sure there isn't anywhere else we could go?"

"Everything else was full," you say. "This was the only place left. Plus, a gay guy. I thought it would be gorgeous. I thought there would be flowers."

"In March?"

"Daffodils," you say. "I wanted everything to be perfect."

"It is perfect," Claire says. "I'm with you." She kisses your nose.

"You're sweet," you say.

Claire says, "This place might be bearable mid-summer. I mean, at least we wouldn't be stuck indoors."

"The view is nice," you say bravely. The bay has filled with late afternoon fog, pierced through with shafts of lustrous sunlight. Even in your room, you can smell salt in the air overtop the faint odor of dirty—what? Shoes? Sheets? The rocks in the shallows are distantly blue, and you can hear sea lions braying.

Claire thumbs through a book on killer whales. She reads out a description of an orca grabbing a seal by the tail and pounding it so hard against the waves that the seal slams out of its skin.

To you, that sounds like cancer. It pounded you so hard against the waves your breast slammed out of your skin and you barked like a seal. Just be glad you have pain receptors. The surgery hurt you. You can't yet sleep on your stomach or side and you can't get comfortable on your back.

First thing this morning, you had to stop at your surgeon's to have your seroma drained. A seroma is a build-up of fluid against your chest wall, but its name reminds you of a disco song: My Seroma! The doctor aimed a syringe the size of Seattle at your chest and sunk the needle. Bloody fluid filled the canister. Claire held your hand, gasping her shock. But thank god for small miracles: You felt nothing, because at the surgery site you are numb, numb, numb, your nerves severed.

After the doctor there was the race to Horseshoe Bay, then the wait at the ferry terminal because the first boat was full. Then came the fuel-stinking ferry itself, its food bland and unappetizing, its coffee weak as water, its strangers with their tales of woe.

You passed a grocery store with goats grazing on its roof.

You barely lifted your head for Cathedral Grove where a stand of old growth trees were bisected by the highway.

"Do we get to drive through one?" you asked blinking awake.

Claire said, "This is Canada, silly."

After that, there was four-hour drive across the island, snow in the mountain passes, plenty of it, and cars off the road. You were really wrung out.

Claire informs you that exploring tidal pools can be dangerous. "There can be rouge waves."

"Rogue waves?"

"Rouge waves," she corrects. "It says so right here." She holds out the book.

It's true. It says rouge waves not once but three times, surely no typo. You wonder what would happen if you and Claire were tickling a sea anemone, its cat-tongue tentacles closing around your fingers, and got struck by a rouge wave. Certainly you'd look healthier, less like a cancer crip. Perhaps there are other helpful waves too. Peaks on the Pectorals rouge waves. Face lift rouge waves.

"We got hit by a real mascara out there," you could tell your mother during your weekly call.

Phantom boob pain. You can't scratch, but you are going insane. Claire tries to help, tracing ribbons of dead skin down your arm, across your back, but she can't reach the itch. She even tries scratching the air where your breast used to be.

"Let's go get something to eat," she finally says. "Let's blow this pop stand."

The restaurant is the Crab Bar. The theme is Sixties nautical with fishnet looped across the ceiling holding dried starfish and shells, and a rowboat suspended over the bar. It's small, dim, crowded; you're shown to a table the size of a plate. You and Claire both order half crabs. You use nutcrackers, rooting around in the reddened shell with skinny forks; you dip the flesh in hot butter and feed each other.

By the end of dinner you find yourself relaxing. You're away from the ever-present worries about having cancer (lumpectomy and radiation? mastectomy? chemo that improves your odds by only 7 percent?), from the cacophony of the city. You suck Claire's finger deep inside your mouth and confide fantasies of romance and raunchy sex, a room strewn with discarded clothing.

"At the House of a Thousand Shag Rugs?" Claire asks. "I know you like dirty sex, but that's going too far even for you."

You grin. You really, really adore this woman. You've been together for years, but it seems, because of the fun you have, because of the way you light up in her presence, like only weeks.

"We'd have to borrow Pine Sol and a mop," says Claire, "before I'd even consider letting you toss my bra on that floor."

"You're wearing a bra?" you ask, breathless, catching her wrist in your hand.

On the way back to the B+B, you have sex in your car, steaming the windows, the roar of the surf pounding in your ears.

"I couldn't bear to lose you," Claire whispers.

"You won't lose me," you say, although this is not what you believe.

"Promise you won't die," Claire says.

But you're mute now, busy. *I promise I won't die,* you think.

You aren't sure how it happens, but you're on your knees, licking, with the fingers of your good hand pushed deep inside where it feels like sand and ocean, when Claire's elbow jams the horn, piercing the night. The two of you can't get the thing to go off; you punch it and fiddle with wire under the dash, but it keeps blaring. A Pacific Rim park ranger shines his light in the driver's window, his face spectral above it. You are tugging on clothes, except with one arm gimp you still need help dressing. Claire yanks her shirt across her breasts.

"It won't go off," Claire says, rolling down the window with one hand as she struggles to get her pants around her hips with the other.

The ranger reaches under the dash just like you did, but for him the noise ceases. "You'd be surprised," he says enigmatically. "Do you two have a parking pass? You have to pay to park here. Twenty-four seven."

Neither of you says anything. Winded, you hold your coat up to cover the spot where your breast used to be. You worry you've popped your incision.

"I'm going to have to write you up."

You look down, but it's too dark to tell if you're leaking blood.

The man scribbles, then passes a ticket through the window, tips his hat and says, "Have a good evening, ladies."

Just be glad you have an incision.

There is no sign of Skip or his mangy dog back at The House of a Thousand Pubic Hairs on the Bathroom Floor. You pull snowy ter-rycloth robes from the closet. You vacillate—nude?—and settle, for their possible protective value, on suits. You hold hands across the veranda and regard the hot tub. It smells like decaying vegetable mat-ter. When Claire sheds the complimentary robe, she pulls a condom wrapper from her pocket. Gingerly, you dip your hand into yours and pull up used, calcified tissues.

Claire shivers with disgust. "The sooner we go to sleep," she says, "the sooner we'll be up and out of this shit hole."

First, though, you have to use the communal washroom. Before crawling between the inexplicably clean sheets, you try to lock the patio door but it jams open, a cold sliver of March wind whistling through the drapes. You settle into bed, kissing Claire as if your life depends on it.

Just be glad you have lips.

Late that night, you are wakened by Skip settling new guests in the room beside you. You can hear every word they say as they urgently discuss the man's father's hernia operation, what stuck out where. They discuss operations. You roll into Claire, who holds you, careful of your arm.

In the morning, the couple next door make love. As far as you can tell, there is not a lot of what heterosexuals call foreplay; their beds slams against the wall behind your heads and you jiggle. When the man comes, he repeatedly grunts. The woman doesn't come at all, as far as you can tell, but she does cry out that she loves him.

"Good," he says back. As in: Good sex.

"Do you love *me*?" she asks. There's a pause, then she says, "Drew? Drew? Are you asleep? Wake up, honey."

"Claire," you whisper, "we have to get out of here. I know everything's booked, but we can't spend another day here." You imagine going hotel to hotel, looking for cancellations.

"We could go home," Claire says.

But Vancouver seems as distant as Paris or Rome. And anyhow, the Cancer Agency is waiting with cyclophosphomide, 5FU and methotrexate. You don't want to go back. Not yet. You shake your head.

"We can't have breakfast here. I'll take you to town," Claire says.

When you pull back the plastic-coated drapes, it is sunny and gorgeous; the hummingbirds are already feeding.

You tiptoe upstairs to get a glass of water for your pain medications; the new couple introduces themselves as Trudy and Drew, from Chemainus. They are both high school science teachers, Trudy tells you.

"We collect Teachable Moments," she says with a little toss of her hair and a giggle.

"TMs," Drew says, "that we can share with our students back home. We're planning to do a unit on mammals of the sea."

Skip calls out, "Coffee or tea? I'm scrambling eggs."

You stand in the kitchen door and politely decline. "We have to go," you say. "So sorry, but we can't stay."

Skip doesn't have a dishwasher; last night's supper dishes swim in a sink of scummy water. Islands of beige, solidified fat skim across them.

"Can I please have a glass?" you ask.

"You paid to eat here," Skip says, his voice thick.

"My sweetie wants to take me out." You make your way to the sink and run water into your palm, from which you slurp.

Skip cracks an egg and turns to face you. His eyes, blue and rheumy, are actually damp. Is it possible he can't see the filth? "Oh, please?" he says. "Pretty please with a cherry on top?"

"Um," you say.

"It would mean so much."

In the dining room, Trudy messes with a telescope. Drew moves behind her and twines his arms around her.

"Scan the horizon nice and slow," he says. "That's it, honey. Nice and slow."

Trudy tilts the telescope past the sheltered bay towards open water.

"Twenty thousand grey whales migrate past here every spring," Drew tells you. "Also, there are thirty to forty resident whales."

"I see a blow!" Trudy cries.

You can see blows even without binoculars, but you don't say anything. Grey whales—big deal, you think. Rocks with fountains. Not that you've ever seen one up close. You came through here with an ex, once, and went out on one of the Canadian Pacific boats. Drenched, cold, the closest you came to a whale sighting was the gunwale. Still, you're willing to try again for Claire's sake.

Trudy crows, "TM!" and she and Drew both laugh.

Claire wanders upstairs and puts her chin on your shoulder. Skip says, "Tea's ready, everyone," and carries in a tray of steaming mugs. There is a Tweetie Bird mug and one from Tim Hortons, a Charles and Di wedding mug. Considering the princess's long ago death, you wouldn't imagine this mug would be happily evocative, but it makes Trudy gush, makes her tell you about William and Kate, and then that Drew proposed on the beach the night before.

Claire says, "Well, congratulations." She turns helplessly to you. "Weren't we on our way out?"

You explain that Skip had already started breakfast. But what you're thinking is that if Drew and Trudy just got engaged, why on earth were they discussing hernias? Why, also, did she have to beg him to tell her he loves her? You say, "Claire and I have been married for seven years."

Trudy's face furrows. "Married?" she says.

Trudy gasps. "Are you guys *lesbians?*"

"TM!" you chirp. This was why you became a lesbian—to be someone's Teachable Moment. You think, Just be glad you have a ring finger.

Claire puts her head down on the table. You are helplessly, head-over-the-heels-you-aren't-glad-you-have in love with Claire. Claire is equally smitten with you, so that you often moon, pie-eyed, staring at each other with considerably more gusto than Drew and Trudy muster up. Like many lesbians, you have had a series of pathetic relationships, and Claire arrived when you had given up hoping. Yet because things are so good between you, tension has always ridden just under the surface like a diving whale. At any moment tragedy could intervene, pulling you apart. Pulling happiness to bits. You convinced Claire you needed a burglar alarm to keep you safe, then after it was installed, found your lump while you were in the shower.

Claire was opening a mail order package from Wichita, Kansas.

"I have a lump," you said.

"A lump?" Claire asked distractedly. She unwrapped a beer mug and held it up to the light.

"In my right breast."

"I didn't order beer mugs," Claire said. "I ordered a down vest."

"I'm making a doctor's appointment," you said.

Claire said, "I can't believe this. There are eight beer mugs here." But then she looked at you. Finally it hit her. You watched it hit her, watched it reach out and strike her like a fist.

Now Drew wants to know if you two are going whale watching. Claire sits back up, apparently reconciled to breakfast. "We were planning to go in a zodiac," he says, as Trudy swoons into his side, "but last weekend a Swedish couple died."

Because he is a teacher, he is the only one who hears news reports.

"A rouge wave swamped them," Claire says.

Trudy blinks and turns to Drew for interpretation.

"Honey, I think she means rogue," Drew says under his breath.

"Think of it this way," Claire says. "If we go down, they can make Zodiac, the Movie. Kind of a west coast Titanic."

The dog hops into the great room wagging its intermittently bushy tail. Skip slips plates heaving with bright orange eggs in front of each of you. He says, "If you sign up with Island Adventures, I'll be your captain."

"You take your guests whale watching?"

"There's a five percent discount for the lovely honeys who stay at The House of a Thousand Flowers," he says. For some reason, his pudgy hand is circling ever so slowly around his stomach which this morning is, thank heavens, covered. "I always save a session just for my guests. I'll bet you find all the other outfits are booked up with those fooey psychiatrists."

You look at Claire. She looks at you. You push the food around the plate. There is a bit of calcified egg yolk still on the rim from who knows when. From what poor guests.

When Skip leaves, Trudy whispers, "That dog has mange. He should have put it down."

"It seems okay," Claire observes. She holds out her plate down so the dog can eat up her eggs.

"I don't agree with people keeping disabled pets," Trudy says. "That dog could infect someone."

Drew says, "Trudy."

She pops a hand over her mouth. "Oops! You have to say, 'Pet with a disability,'" she says. "Not disabled pet. Oops."

Claire looks at you.

You spend the morning begging for alternate accommodations in motel lobbies, even seamy ones, but every room is occupied. You also inquire of several adventure travel operations about whale watching, but they are, as Skip predicted, fully booked. You drive to Long Beach, scene of Claire's so slippery thighs. It's wild and rugged, with waves tall as pine trees foaming onto the beach. Sandpipers toothpick along like upside down hor d'oeuvres. Claire, rosy-cheeked and utterly healthy, takes your hand and runs you towards the surf, laughing. She is rosy-cheeked and utterly healthy. Surfers in neoprene jog towards the water with boards Velcroed to their ankles.

You clamber up a rock exposed by low tide. Clouds hang like flagstones over your head, low and heavy. Although it was washily sunny, now it's bordering on rain. Tide pools bristle with life—brown and crusty sea cucumbers shaped like flaccid penises; shockingly bright starfish, orange and purple, that ooze like sandbags; anemones in tones of gentle greens and pinks. The rocks are thick with barnacles. Everywhere, everywhere, is water. It laps up on the shore, spits the air, seeps through the sand below. The ocean is blue, cavernous, but with the sun behind clouds it turns green and forbidding. Not the noxious green of Skip's carpet. Not tropical postcard green, but a northern green, as if it had dissolved a forest of Douglas fir.

The marina is also a grocery store. And a cappuccino bar. Beside you, Drew orders a skinny latte on a leash.

"Are you sure you want to do this?" Claire asks when the girl behind the counter at Island Adventures passes you a waver. The outfit is not responsible for a) accidental death or b) accidental dismemberment or c) people born without heels. This is all at your own risk. If a rouge wave takes you, you're on your own. If you die of hypothermia, possible here even in midsummer, tough noogies. You hear the insufferable if orgasmic Drew explaining to Trudy that a skinny latte on a leash is actually a cup of coffee with steamed milk to go and that he got it for her because with anything else, she might gain weight.

If the boat capsizes, you may die during one of Drew's Teachable Moments, you realize. Are there worse things? You've already left your breast behind in a laboratory sliced into sections, purple dye rimming the tissue where once the tumour rested, and your lymph nodes like fleshy diamonds. Maybe there are worse things. Dying long and slow of breast cancer. And anyway, think of the press. Think of the Chemainus high school students boning up on rouge waves for the memorial service.

You meet down on the docks near the Canadian Princess cruise ship, now a floating hotel, which swarms with shrinks in dark clothing pointing in all directions toward water. This is where you stayed when you came here with your ex. The two of you had a whopper of a fight, hollering at each other through a port hole about why she'd been hours late getting home from work for three weeks running (Gracie, the woman's name was Gracie), and then went whale watching still furious. You didn't have a raincoat. You got soaked to the bone then spilled boiling hot chocolate across your new Mabel League baseball jersey.

You have a hard time believing that Skip is going to be your captain, but there he is on deck, rotund, grey, scab-legged. He says, "Ahoy, adorable maties," and throws out orange survival suits like lifesavers. The dog hops along the deck and jumps in the boat, her tongue lolling out the side of her mouth. Boats creak against cushioning rubber tires affixed to the docks; seagulls whirl through the sky. The zodiac itself it hardly the size of a Volkswagen bug. Yellow, it sloshes up and down on top of the waves. The survival suits are padded from shoulder to ankle and in them, you and Claire, and Drew and Trudy, look like Michelin Men, or obscene orange marshmallows. Drew says the survival suits will keep you warm for twenty minutes, tops, and that you'll be doomed in an accident if help doesn't arrive quickly.

You consider telling him you are doomed anyhow.

He tells you that sharks sometimes attack surfboarders, mistaking them for seals. He launches into a long speech on the feeding habits of great whites.

"TM," Trudy giggles.

"F-O," Claire mutters.

You know what she means.

You putter around the end of the dock, past grizzled fishing boats drawing nets onto huge spools.

"Hold on, babies," Skip calls once you're past the last, as he increases the throttle.

You almost fall off the bench seat, almost go spilling into the cold Pacific. Claire steadies your elbow.

Drew says something about thrust.

Skip slows down to tour you past a colony of honking sea lions, behemoths who could fit two of themselves inside their loose folds of skin. Several of them, alarmed by the zodiac, glide into the water with surprising gracefulness, but there is one atop a low rock that barely raises its head.

"That big boy there is pooping out," Skip yells.

You are positive the sea lion, his eyes limpid and brown, makes contact with you, that the two of you communicate in the special language of dying animals, saying something profound to each other like: "Shit." Just be glad you have an anus.

Skip throttles up and you rocket away from the sea lion's fate. It is a lot like a ride at an amusement park; you leave the water, bullet through the air, then slam back down in the lee between monster waves. Never mind whales; you don't need whales. You find yourself laughing full-throatedly, unselfconsciously, and despite an itch near your chest, you don't think of cancer or being bald or dying a really pathetic death wearing scarves. You just have fun. You have a laff riot. You have a conniption. You have a zoo. You keep getting drenched, but you don't care. You snap off ten shots of your twelve-exposure-throwaway-camera roll just on Claire's delighted face.

Skip stops, letting the zodiac float each wave up and down, up and down. He says there have been whales frequent this area. You don't know how tall the waves actually are, but when you're in one of the valleys, they look about twenty feet higher than you. You have no idea what kind they are, either, rouge, mascara or maybe even lipstick, but does it matter?

Regardless, this is more like it. This is water writ large.

Drew and Trudy, holding binoculars in the front, scan the horizon that's only visible when a wave lifts you high. Drew sees a blow. It is closer than it would be from land, but it is still pretty far off, pretty distant.

Drew turns around to tell you grey whales are baleen feeders who scoop crustaceans from the ocean bottom.

"Thank you," your finger tells his back.

In the second before a wave swallows you, you see the far-off, barnacled arch of a grey whale's back, then the characteristic spout.

Skip calls out that whale breath, up close, stinks as bad as a drag queen's high heels.

You turn around, laughing, but Skip is bent over, picking off a scab.

You bob for another half hour but don't wind up very close to any whales. Still, que sera. It's better than when you came here with your ex. Come to that, your whole life is better. You snake an arm around Claire's back. It's like trying to hold the Pillsbury dough boy, but what the heck. You love her. You're wild about her. You're glad to be in Ucluelet with her, even stuck at The House of a Thousand Unblooming Fagots.

Trudy spots a number of blows towards land. She and Drew and Skip train their binoculars. You, however, stare at Claire whose eyes are dancing with pleasure. That's why you and you alone see the whale spy-hopping beside the zodiac, perhaps ten feet out, nearly close enough to touch, its amazing barnacle-encrusted snout, its long, open mouth with the small, blunt teeth and finally the black, lightless eye which pokes above the wave.

"Turn around slowly," you mouth to Claire, and she does.

Time hangs like a curtain, unruffled and unmoving. The sun parts the clouds and beats down on your hair. Claire, to her credit, doesn't gasp. She just seeks out your hand and squeezes it immensely hard, hard enough so that it will hurt later. You don't mind. You couldn't mind anything in this moment, eyeballing a grey whale in the middle of the Pacific Ocean. You can't believe how silent the encounter is. You can't believe that Drew, Trudy and Skip don't see it. It's your own Teachable Moment, the one that exists for just you and Claire. You don't even think to take a picture. But a fist unclenches in your chest, and you realize something that lies under the pain of being so sick: You are really, truly glad you have heels.

The whale blinks, then subsides below the surface like a periscope. Glad, glad, oh how happy you are to have body parts at all.

Jane Eaton Hamilton is the author of seven books including the poetry title Love Will Burst into a Thousand Shapes *(2014). She has won many awards for her fiction, including, twice, first prize in the CBC Literary Awards, Canada's most prestigious short fiction contest.*

FROG LEGS

Michael Craft

Amateur night—that's what they called it back in college, back when he was learning to drink. New Year's Eve—the night of resolutions and fresh beginnings. Now, though, in the last year of his fifties, there would be far less drinking, tepid interest in resolutions, and no chance whatever that he would be awake for the ritual flipping of the calendar.

Marson Miles, AIA, an architect at the height of his modestly esteemed career, stood in his dressing room, his sanctuary, in the house he had designed but hated. Were it not for his wife, their home would reflect the clean, disciplined aesthetic that had inspired his design of the local performing-arts complex. Questman Center had wowed critics and public alike at its dedication the prior spring and had been featured as a cover story in the autumn issue of *ArchitecAmerica*, the first such coup to be scored during the thirty-year practice of Miles & Norris LLP.

"Marson?"

"Yes, Precious?" He turned from the framed magazine cover, which was not permitted to be displayed in the public areas of the house, and offered a feeble smile to his wife, who had banished the hard-won trophy to his closet.

"Zip me," she said with a clumsy pirouette, showing him her back, from which sagged the glittery flaps of a too-tight cocktail dress.

"Yes, Precious." He called her Precious; friends called her Prue; her parents had called her Prucilla. He zipped her, lamenting her choice of couture, which might have looked comely on a woman half her age—a woman old enough to be their daughter. But there were no children. They had tried, at first, but the lack of offspring had been met with little more than a mutual shrug, so they gave up. And in time, without rancor, without even much discussion, they had fallen into their arrangement of separate beds—in separate bedrooms.

His suite was a tranquil island of minimalism, with spare, contemporary furnishings and a subdued, neutral palette, while her suite wallowed in a florid outpouring of the posh Tudor aesthetic that enshrouded the mini-mansion she had badgered him into building for her. One day during the construction phase, in the offices of Miles & Norris, he had glanced over the floor plans, shaking his head. "It's a Disney monstrosity, replete with turrets," he said to Ted Norris, who was not only Marson's business partner, but also Prucilla's brother. "All that's missing is a drawbridge and a moat."

Tonight in Marson's closet, Prucilla eyed her husband askance. "You're wearing *that?*"

"I think so, yes." For their New Year's Eve dinner with Ted and Peg Norris, Marson had dressed in classic, understated good taste— black cashmere blazer, charcoal flannel slacks, white spread-collar shirt, and *the* tie. Of the hundreds of neckties arranged by color and pattern, hung from carousel hooks on both sides of a full-length mirror, his trusty old Armani provided the finishing touch for most special occasions. Silvery gray damask, with a subtle pattern of jaunty geometrics, it was both dressy and sporty, coordinating with almost anything. He couldn't recall exactly when he had bought it, at least twenty years ago, but it had cost some two hundred dollars, even then.

A shameless extravagance, to be sure—but oh, the silk, the hand, the way it tied—*this* is what they meant when they spoke of investment dressing.

She watched with a snarky frown as he stood before the mirror, looping and sliding the sinuous tails of silk, which began to form the distinctive V-shaped Windsor knot beneath his throat. She said, "If you insist on wearing that old thing, can't you at least have it cleaned?"

"It's clean, Precious. I take good care of my things. Besides, you can't dry-clean a necktie."

"Don't be ridiculous."

He glanced over his shoulder at her. "Have you ever tried it?"

"Well, *no.*"

"I have." He returned his attention to the mirror, explaining, "They come back clean, but the body or the sizing or whatever—it's shot. They never tie right again. No, the only thing to do with a soiled necktie is to throw it out." Marson gave a final tug, pinched the knot with a perfect dimple, and watched as the tip of the Armani dropped precisely over his belt buckle. He spun on his heel to face her and raised both palms, intoning, "Tuh-dah!"

She mimicked his gesture, then scowled as she tossed her palms toward him. "Don't forget," she said, marching out of the closet and into the hall, "we're five tonight."

"Don't remind me." He followed. "I'm not sure what to think of your nephew's arrival."

She halted under a velvet-swagged iron chandelier and turned. "You *hired* him."

"The job offer was your brother's idea. Things are picking up, and we could use the help, so I went along with it."

"See? Everything's hunky-dory." Her tone turned menacing: "So what's the problem?"

He shrugged. "It's just that I hardly know Brody. How old was he—like *fourteen?*" The Brody in question was the son of Inez Norris, older sister of both Marson's wife, née Prucilla Norris, and Marson's business partner, Ted Norris. Something of a black sheep, Inez had followed her hippie leanings to California and, even now, remained estranged from the family, although she had returned for Marson and Prucilla's wedding thirty-five years ago, single and pregnant—with Brody. Marson's only other, postnatal, sighting of Brody had been fourteen years later, when Ted married Peg.

Recalling this, Marson realized that Ted's wedding, his second, had been the occasion for which Marson had bought his pet tie, the Armani. He had stood as best man. And at the reception, he'd met Brody.

"He *was* fourteen," Marson said to Prucilla, astonished by the passage of time. "And now he's an architect . . . and he's coming to work for me . . . and we've barely met."

She leaned close, speaking low. "You'll meet him tonight. Think of it as a family reunion." Her breath smelled of cucumber as she fingered his tie. "Happy New Year, Marson."

A drop of something hot and acidic slid to the pit of his stomach.

A star-pierced sky arched over the frigid night. There'd been a dusting of snow for Christmas, but it was gone now, and the dry, thin air felt clean and invigorating to Marson as he crossed the restaurant parking lot with Prucilla. He hadn't bothered with a topcoat; she huddled into a black mink cape while pecking across the asphalt, sputtering puffs of steam, churning her arms like the pistons of an old locomotive.

As they entered the restaurant lobby on the stroke of eight (Marson was nothing if not punctual), diners from the early-bird seating doddered out, while those who would be reveling at midnight were still at home dressing, drinking, or both. The hostess looked up from her computer and stepped over to greet them. "Don't you look *special* tonight. Happy New Year."

"Thank you, Connie," said Prucilla, pivoting her shoulders so Connie could remove the fur.

"Same to you, Connie," said Marson. "Have the Norrises arrived?"

"About two minutes ago." Connie draped the mink over one arm; with the other, she gestured toward the far end of the dining room. "You've got the prime booth tonight, number twenty-two. You folks enjoy." And with a bob of her head, she hustled the fur away.

Marson took Prucilla's arm to guide her past the bar and through the crowded room, but she pulled it back. Though they had often dined here and always liked it, New Year's could be an ordeal. Booked to capacity, the room was not only noisier than usual, but decorated with a cloud of gold and silver balloons that floated about the ceiling, trailing Mylar streamers that swayed at eye level. And there would be a special menu—overblown, overpriced.

Prucilla gave a demure wave as they plodded through the crowd. From the side of her mouth, she told Marson, "I don't know *what* Ted sees in Peg. Talk about mousy."

"Now, now—she always speaks kindly of *you*," he lied.

Booth twenty-two was horseshoe-shaped, with a round table, surveying the entire room from the far corner, backed by mirrored walls. The combined effect of the mirrors and the fluttering Mylar made Marson feel unsure on his feet—and he hadn't had a drink yet. Brody had not arrived, but Ted and Peg were seated together at the back of the horseshoe, watching and smiling. As their friends drew near, they began to inch toward the ends of the booth, sliding and squeaking on the leatherette, preparing to stand.

With a laugh, Marson waved them down. "Stay put—it's 'just us.'" Greeted with cheery handshakes and air-kisses, the new arrivals settled in at the ends of the horseshoe, Marson next to Ted, with Prucilla next to Peg. It was a tight fit. Marson wondered if Brody was not joining them after all—or if he was, where he would sit.

Prucilla was telling Peg, "Love your little frock ..."

Marson asked Ted, "Did, uh, Brody's flight get in okay?"

Ted nodded. "Last night. He did some exploring today. He'll need a place to live—hell, he's starting a whole new life. He'll be here soon." Ted flashed Marson a quiet smile that transcended four decades. Their wives dished the dirt.

A round of drinks arrived. They had known each other so long, Ted had already placed the order: bourbon for himself, a dry gin martini for Marson, chardonnay for Peg, and a champagne cocktail for Prucilla. They were in the middle of a generic toast, something about "us" and "the future" and "new beginnings," when Marson's eye drifted to the mirror behind Ted, in which he saw Connie approaching with a chair hoisted overhead, leading someone to the table. Before Marson could turn and stand to greet their guest, Connie had planted the chair in the opening of the horseshoe and—bang—there sat Brody.

Amid the clatter of arranging a new place setting and ordering the fifth drink, amid the welcomes and the musings about the passing of years, Marson marveled at the transformation of the gangly fourteen-year-old he had met so long ago. Now in his mid-thirties, Brody Norris had flowered into an intelligent and affable young man who also happened to be an architect of considerable promise—and jaw-droppingly handsome. Peg's jaw did in fact drop as she hung on his every word, while Prucilla listened with a look of forced enthusiasm, as if miffed that *this* had sprung from the loins of her sister non grata.

As for Marson, his singular reaction to Brody's *beauty*—which was indeed the right word—was the conspicuous resemblance to Ted Norris in his earlier years. That tousled shock of sandy-blond hair … the crooked grin … those arresting green eyes. With Brody to the right and Ted to the left, Marson glanced back and forth, seeing two men, nephew and uncle, who looked more like twin brothers at different ages. Yes, there were some knockout genes in the Norris family. To Prucilla's misfortune, though, their transmission had been restricted to the Y chromosomes.

Brody wagged his hands in a halting gesture. "Before we say an-other word"—the chitchat subsided—"I just need to tell Marson that I could *not* have been more impressed with Questman Center. Sure, I'd seen the piece in *ArchitecAmerica*, but the photos didn't begin to capture what I saw this afternoon. I took the tour—"

Marson interrupted, "Thanks, Brody, but—"

"I took the tour," Brody continued, resting his fingertips on the sleeve of Marson's blazer, "and I couldn't help thinking, My God, this is right up there with the best of Mies, Corbu, Neutra—you name it. Sure, the term has gone threadbare, but Questman truly is *iconic*."

"Agreed," said Ted, raising his glass. "Bravo, Marson."

Marson reminded his partner, "Your name's on it, too. We're a team."

Ted told his nephew, "Don't listen to him. Marson's the designer. I mind the business and the engineering."

Marson laughed. "I need *somebody* to make sure the roof stays up."

Brody touched Marson's arm again. "Well, I was totally blown away, and so were the docents this afternoon when I told them I was coming to work for you."

"Frog legs!" said Prucilla.

All heads turned to her.

She waved the evening's menu card. "It's a prix fixe, and the ap-petizer is frog legs."

"Ish," said Peg. Prucilla was right—Peg *was* mousy. She spoke lit-tle, so when she did, people took note.

"Well, I think that sounds rather *festive*," said Ted, nudging his wife.

"I've never had them," said Marson, "but it's New Year's, and there's a first time for everything."

By the time the appetizer arrived, the table was on its second round of drinks, and any squeamishness Marson might have felt about the frogs was quelled by the gin.

"Tastes like chicken," said Peg.

"They say the same thing about rattlesnake," said Prucilla, chowing down.

Ted brought the focus back to Brody: "So ... when did things fall apart with Lloyd?"

Brody set a bone on the plate and dabbed his lips with a napkin. "It started a year ago. I knew something was up when he needed to be traveling over Christmas. I mean, his kids are *my* age, and they'd always come to California, but last year—supposedly—he needed to visit *them*. Turns out he went to Vegas, to meet this guy we'd done a beach house for in Malibu. Five years younger than me, lots of bucks—catnip for Lloyd. It took six months to get everything out in the open, then another six to get it settled. But it's over."

Marson asked quietly, "You made out all right?"

Brody nodded. "We were married in California. Now we're divorced. And the firm is closed. Fifty-fifty."

"That's tough," said Marson, "but I'm glad you had those protections in place."

Brody smiled. "And I'm glad I landed here."

"How nice," said Prucilla, licking her fingers. "Everybody's glad and happy." The sauce was Asian, sweet, and sticky.

Ted said, "Amazing, isn't it, how times have changed? The whole 'gay issue' is so mainstream now."

"How modern," said Prucilla. "Everybody's so open and evolved."

Ted turned to Marson. "Remember, back in college? The topic was sort of ... *radical*."

Marson's brows arched. "Was it ever."

With a quizzical look, Brody asked, "You guys went to college together?"

"Sure," said Ted. "Architecture school—that's how we met."

Marson added, "We were roommates."

The table went silent for a moment.

Prucilla cleared her throat, then leaned to tell Peg in a stage whisper, "It makes one wonder if there might have been some antics in the dorm."

Peg's eyes bugged.

Brody laughed. "Nonsense, Aunt Prue. I have special powers—that gaydar thing? And I can tell you with absolute certainty that Uncle Ted is utterly, *incorrigibly* heterosexual."

Ted lifted his hands in surrender. "Guilty as charged."

"*I'll* tell the world," said Peg, nuzzling him.

And at that moment, under the table, a table that squeezed five people into the space for four, Brody's knee drifted a microscopic distance toward Marson's, and as the woolen fibers of their slacks approached each other in the dry air of a January's eve, a spark—an actual spark of static electricity—leapt from one leg to the other with a sharp, audible snap that shot through Marson's thigh and made him gasp.

"Gosh, sorry," said Brody, moving his knee. Then he eased it back again, letting it rest against Marson's.

Breathless, Marson dared not let his eyes meet anyone else's. Staring down at the plate of stripped-clean frog bones—long, thin, and delicate, they didn't resemble chicken at all—he felt suddenly nauseated by the thought of having eaten this swamp thing, and he saw the array of bones circling the table, circling the entire dining room, and he wondered what they did with the *rest* of the frogs, and he envisioned a dumpster behind the restaurant brimming with these bloated, legless swamp things, and he wasn't feeling well at all, and he regretted that second martini, and he was *very* concerned about that egg-and-spinach thing for lunch, and—

"Marson!" said Prucilla, aghast.

"Precious?"

"You're white as a sheet. What's *wrong* with you?" Her tone was more scolding than concerned.

Brody touched Marson's hand and looked into his eyes. "Are you okay?"

"Um"—Marson blotted his forehead, then his lips, and set the napkin on the banquette—"sorry. I just need a bit of air. Excuse me, please."

Brody got up and moved his chair aside.

Marson edged out of the booth, composed himself, and mustered a nonchalant air as he made his way across the dining room toward the lobby. Passing by Connie, he explained, "Forgot something in the car," and went out the front door.

In the parking lot, he found a quiet corner, leaned over a bush to brace one palm against the wall, and took a long, deep breath of the night air. For a moment he thought the nausea might pass. But he was wrong. And dangling beneath him in the cold breeze, directly in the path of the gushing, greasy frog bile, was his favorite Armani necktie.

New Year's morning, the house was quiet, save for the lullaby rumble of the furnace.

Marson awoke with a clear head and a calm stomach—the silver lining to his purge the prior night. Having had no appetite for dinner, he was now hungry, so he decided to spiff up for a nice brunch somewhere. He showered and shaved, made a few phone calls, and dressed for the day in velvety corduroys, a comfy lambswool V-neck, and smart Italian loafers.

With the folded, sullied necktie in hand, he went down to the kitchen. Its walls had the texture of rough-hewn stone (faux, of course), like a dungeon from some cheesy production of *The Pit and the Pendulum*. But this morning the room seemed bright to him, bright with the prospect of change.

Prucilla sat with a cup of coffee in a shaft of sunlight at the breakfast table, reading a newspaper, nibbling toast. She wore a tentlike flannel housecoat and a spongy pink turban. Facing the window, she made no acknowledgment that Marson had entered the room, despite the distinct clack of his loafers on the limestone floor.

He stepped to the sink, opened the door to the trash bin, and tossed in the Armani, where it settled among the coffee grounds. Closing the door, he asked, "Why did you marry me?"

Her head made the slightest turn in his direction. Her lips sputtered with a chortle that sent toast crumbs darting through the beam of sunlight. Then her gaze returned to the paper.

He moved to the table and sat across from her. His voice was soft but sure: "It was a serious question. It deserves an answer."

She set down the paper, sipped her coffee, and paused in thought, eyes adrift. "What's the stock answer—'love'? Let's just say I married you for the same reasons you married me."

"I doubt that," he told her. "You see, I married *you* because I was deeply—and impossibly—in love with your brother."

For the first time that morning, she looked at him.

He continued, "I married *you* to keep Ted in my life. The business came later."

Her features pinched, then relaxed. "Feel better? Get it off your chest?"

"Prucilla"—he never called her that—"I want out."

She laughed. "Want out? I'll suck you dry and *spit* you out."

He looked about, whirled his hands. "It's all just . . . *stuff.* You can have it."

"Then it's true what they say: there's no fool like an old fool."

"Maybe." He knew it was an odd moment to be smiling. Patting a pocket for his keys, he said, "I need to be going."

"Where?"

"Brunch. At the club."

"How dreary. Why would you go to New Year's brunch *solo*?"

He paused. "I'm not."

And beneath the table, Marson relived the sense memory of Brody's knee touching his.

And he felt the spark.

Michael Craft is the author of more than a dozen published novels and two produced plays. Three of his Mark Manning *mystery novels have been honored as national finalists for Lambda Literary Awards. He holds an MFA in creative writing from Antioch University, Los Angeles, and lives in Rancho Mirage, California. Visit the author's website at www.michaelcraft.com.* 'Frog Legs' *has been previously published in* Chelsea Station Magazine, May 2014, Chelsea Station Editions, *and* Badlands Literary Journal, Fall 2014, California State University, San Bernardino, Palm Desert Campus.

JAMIE

Dawn Munro

Remember me when I am gone away,
Gone far away into the silent land;
When you can no more hold me by the hand
Nor I half turn to go yet turning stay
Remember me when no more day by day
You tell me of our future that you planned
Only remember me.

– Christine Rossetti

It could have been the AIDS Walk planned for Philadelphia, Mum's anniversary or even my conversation with Charlene about why her son Daryl, a gifted musician, was dead, that started it off: Charlene had sat on the bench with me at the vigil. She spoke with such bitterness about the pain of her loss as we remembered all the people we'd known, and those whom we hadn't, who had passed on. It started me thinking about the things that I'd blotted out. There are times when

I can be just too cold, too detached and too professional. Then, I go on to regret it with great anguish.

I'd just turned off the expressway when the trembling started. I pulled over, parked and began to walk aimlessly in the soft blackness in the warehouse wastelands down by the river. As I walked, the entire episode came flooding back with a horrific intensity. Sometimes it feels as if I'm walking through molasses: it's an effort to function when I'm this tired. The sleepless nights follow long, working days, and after seventy-two hours, I'm close to losing it. Through my exhaustion and with my nostrils still full of the pervasive smell of feces, I find my mind drifting back to how this all started.

I remember the nights spent sitting in a cramped, overheated, stuffy room, the air thick with the smell of over-boiled coffee and stale cigarette smoke, waiting for my shift to begin. The street sounds penetrate into the room: the sound of a breaking bottle, a harsh yell of "C'mon you bastard," a shrill scream, running feet, and then, in the distance, the wail and howl of the patrol car answering the call. The car's blue, flashing lights, diffused by the frosted glass windows, flood the call room with an eerie light.

It's just another Friday night in the city and, at exactly seven o'clock, the phone shrills in my ear. Here we go again. The litany of despair seems unending. Most of the time the problem is not real, but rather, it's the thinking that is problematical. Even so, for my clients, the perception is reality. There are always one or two real problems and it is in those that the real satisfaction lies; the opportunity to touch someone's life for a little while, to carry their load and, in so doing, to just maybe change something.

This is where it all began, and here I am now, on a grey winter's morning, exhausted, eyes gritty from the lack of sleep, sitting, and watching from the window as the street lights start to go out. The last months have worn me out: the endless battle to get enough nourishment into him to try to stop the weight loss, the oral problems, the bouts of scabies, and the never-ending mountains of laundry. It seems to pile up faster than I can get it washed and dried.

I sip my coffee and look at the heap of bottles, dressing packs and boxes in front of me. I wearily begin to sift through the pile of Acyclovir eye drops, AZT, Rifater, Cimetidine, Azithromycin, Itraconazole, Chlorpheneniramine, Trimethoprim, Pyrixidine, Acyclovir, Piriton, Diazepam, Ketoconazole, and Co-Codamol to find what I need for the eight a.m. medication. I sit confused, experiencing a momentary panic—there are only twenty tablets and capsules and there should be twenty-one. Oh yes, the Nystatin lozenges for the thrush. I wonder how many of them are therapeutic, how many are prophylactic and if the side effects are really worth it?

I sigh to myself, thinking how pointless this is and how it didn't have to end up this way. This boy, like so many others, was desperate for love but had to settle for lust and life as a hustler. How was it that all his friends and lovers had suddenly vanished once it became known that he was, to use the accepted gay euphemism, "sick"?

Looking through the open door to the bedroom I see that the thin, wasted figure is sleeping fitfully now. His face is heavily stubbled and the darkly shadowed eyes which never fully close are deeply sunken; the lesion-pocked skin, paper-thin, is drawn taut across his emaciated face; and I am loath to disturb him. Nights tend not to be too restful. One difficult night the previous week, we'd hugged and talked slowly and painfully about death and what it meant to us. I'd asked him if there was anyone he needed to talk to, and after some beating about the bush, he admitted that he wanted to talk to a minister or priest. The panic having been resolved, he'd drifted back to sleep. I'd anticipated this and had called Frank Docherty, a local Catholic priest I was acquainted with. He listened to my story and said that he'd be happy to come and talk with James, but he was less happy about James' insistence that I be present when they talked.

The pattern most nights was that he would awaken because he needed the bottle, because he had soiled himself and needed to be changed or, sometimes, because he was hurt, scared or lonely and just needed to be hugged. Although I was desperately tired, I dreaded the thought that he might awaken, call out and not be heard, so it was easier to stay awake.

Now, in the pale, insipid light of a winter's dawn, I looked at James sleeping, gathering the tattered remnants of his failing strength for the next round. Today's goal would be to get through today. As I looked at the huddled figure, I thought about how close we'd become over the last few months. I remembered him saying to me one night that, "It is so strange that we don't need to speak to communicate. You are so different from the nurses. You just seem to know what this feels like." He paused for a while and I could sense what was coming, the forbidden question. He turned toward me and asked quietly, "Don, are you gay or are . . ." He left the question unfinished and I waited a few moments and replied, "No James, I'm not gay." He looked at me for a long time with a quizzical, thoughtful expression and then, slowly, that quiet smile of secret knowing and special understanding played on his face. He snuggled his darkly stubbled cheek down against my chest. I folded my arms around him and held him secure until the harsh, ragged breathing eased in sleep, and the dawn came.

At some point, and I can't identify when that was, it had all changed. I had originally come into this to provide help and support to someone who had been a client and then, a friend. Subtly, insidiously almost, it became more. It could have been the night that I bathed and massaged him, taking pleasure in the way his body moved beneath my hands, in the way his skin softened, and in his obvious delight at being able to wiggle his now unstiffened toes. It could have been the night that I gently washed his penis and applied Vaseline to the dry lesion which caused him such acute discomfort, but which he had been too embarrassed to tell the nurses about. It could have been the night that I told him that I was no longer prepared to wear gloves when working with him. It could have been the first night that he awoke, terrified in the dark, begging me to hold him. I don't know

120

and, anyway, it really doesn't matter. The only thing that does matter is the fact that we grew to love each other in a way, and with an intensity, that I would not have thought possible.

My memories from this time are many, and each is a story in its own right. His gratitude for the simple things amazed me. I awoke one night having fallen asleep to find James out of bed. I scolded him for not using the buzzer that I'd rigged up so he could alert me when he needed help. He explained, simply, that he needed to use his commode and didn't want to wake me, as I needed to sleep too. I remember the occasion when he had insisted, against his physician's advice, that they discharge him from hospital so that we could spend our joint birthdays together, at his home. I decorated his bedroom with brightly colored balloons and "Happy Birthday" banners. I went out and bought a bottle of sparkling wine and a small birthday cake. Upon my return, he met me at the door with a kiss and a hug, freshly showered and shaved and wearing a clean sweatshirt and pants. God only knows where he dredged up the strength for this, an almost superhuman effort for him.

I remember too, the night back in hospital when he finally broke and was ready to quit: when he realized that his life was nearly over and his family and all his erstwhile friends and lovers had abandoned him. He asked me if I knew how to operate the syringe driver. When I replied that I did, he begged me to override the controls and set him free. I took him in my arms and told him that I loved him to bits, but that I could not do something like that. He turned his tear-streaked face to mine and, quite unselfconsciously, we kissed, gently at first and then fiercely in this affirmation of life. We knew in that instant that death was inevitable and very near now, but that together we were going to take it to the limit. I remember how tightly he held me and how beautiful was his smile, as, at peace with himself, he drifted into his first real sleep in days.

As we lay together, I heard a click as the door opened, and, after a moment, a much softer click as it closed. Sometime later, as

James slept, I tiptoed out of the room to leave the ward. I wished "Goodnight" to Louise, the staff nurse on night shift. She was sitting at the ward desk with her back to me. She didn't respond until I persisted with my goodnight. Louise, who had seen and done it all, turned to me, arms tightly folded around herself, her eyes red and puffy, and said, "Oh Don, I'm so very sorry." She reached out and took me in her arms, hugged me and whispered, "Courage pet, courage." I knew what she'd seen, but, knowing well the prejudice that James had experienced and how it had affected him, I no longer cared what anyone thought.

Just after our birthday celebration, I was sitting half asleep in the darkened hospital room when I heard a voice croak urgently, "Don, Don." I replied, "I'm here Jamie, I'm here." "Don, I hurt everywhere. I'm tired." I nodded, unable to speak, and choked for a moment. Then, almost as if in a dream, I heard my voice, now clear and steady, say, "James, my love, it's okay to let go." His eyes closed for a moment and his lips moved soundlessly. Then, his eyes reopened and he looked at me unwaveringly and asked, "Don, will you be here for me, really, all the way?" I smiled at him and replied, "Yes my love, I'll be here for you. I'll hold you in my arms and keep you safe forever." He smiled wanly and whispered, "I'm glad. I'm not so scared now." And then he sank back into the pillows. His lips parted slightly, I leaned over and we kissed slowly, gently and tenderly, our tears mingling on his cheek. He smiled up at me and whispered, "It's really strange how things work out, you know. I'm glad you're not gay; I'd never have known whether you were only here for me because you were. I really do love you, but in another way I wish you were gay and that I'd met you a long time ago, before all this, before life became so complicated. I'd have loved to dance with you to 'Blue Savannah.' It won't be long now. Thanks for everything. If only . . ." the weak voice trailed away. I smiled at him and said, "Another time, James, another place, another life, another me. Who knows, Jamie?" I reached out and ruffled his hair and ran my fingertips down the line of his jaw. His eyelids flickered and reopened, "Don, I'm glad we did our birthdays. It was fun." Then, his eyes closed and James slept.

I sat motionless, looking at the wasted figure, conflicting emotions swaying me one way and then another. We'd gone through this together, knowing that the goal, both hopeful and hopeless, was not life itself, but just one more day. Each day was a victory, albeit pyrrhic. Choked by my tears, I thought to myself, "Oh Christ, please just let it be over."

Much later, surrounded by drips of antibiotics and antifungals and the syringe driver, gently infusing the glucose and opiate mix, I listened to his labored breathing. James, asleep but not sleeping, gave a groan and then a startled yelp. I wondered what dreams, visions or nightmares were flitting through his mind in these last hours. His tortured body convulsed for a moment, and the heavily doped eyes opened: eyes, with deep dark shadows, sunken in the haggard and gaunt hundred-year-old face of a boy who had just turned twenty-six. A cough bubbled moistly somewhere deep in his chest, his fingers tightened round my hand and, in a voice thick with phlegm, James croaked, "Don, Don, are you there?" Although his hearing had failed at this point, I answered, "Yes, James, I'm here. I'll be here always." I then turned on the nightlight and drew a heart, a smiley face and three big Xs on the whiteboard. He grinned weakly, a sad sort of grin. The eyes closed and he began to drift silently away on his morphine cloud into the darkness. I slipped out of my clothes, slid naked under the covers, held him to me with our fingers entwined, and waited for the inevitable.

The monitors told me he still had a fluttery heartbeat. His pulse was faint and he was technically alive. In reality, the James I loved with such a passion had gone. The seemingly endless round of medications had finally come to an end, the horrors of repeated bronchoscopies and lumbar punctures were past, the searing headaches were forever gone, and the constant diarrhea was over. I wondered whether this had all happened by chance or whether I had, in some way, been chosen to play a bit part in this ghastly tragedy. I lay, with all manner of thoughts racing through my mind, willing it to be over, agonizing over my own pain. I felt Jamie's hand soften in mine. The sudden shrieking of the monitor startled me, the door swung open and Dave, the duty medic, rushed in. He didn't comment on the strange situation. He just silenced the alarms and looked at me questioningly. I closed my eyes and shook my head. Dave turned off the monitors, noted the time of death, squeezed my bare shoulder, and said, "I'm so terribly sorry, Don. Stay as long as you want."

I left quietly after about an hour, feeling numb and dazed, and wandered back to my laboratory on the other side of the isolation facility. I sat at my desk, head in my hands, blinded by my tears. A little later, the phone rang. It was John, one of the physicians who had been looking after James and who was a dear friend. "Don, are you okay?" His voice was calm and measured and oh-so-very professional. "Don, I am so very sorry, I know that the two of you were very close." I heard my own voice, hollow and distant, say, "Yes, John, I'm fine. I really am. It's all for the best. He's at peace now. Thanks for calling me. I appreciate everything you did for him."

The reality was so very different: I was most certainly not okay. I was staring wide-eyed into space. I was glad the torment was over, but my heart was breaking. At four-fifteen that morning a part of my soul died. Now I needed someone to cuddle me and a dark corner where I could cry. But there was no one there to hold me, so that night I found myself alone in the warm, velvet darkness, cloaked in my anonymity, wracked by great, wrenching sobs. Maybe now my healing could begin.

Dawn Munro is a biologist, born in the UK who moved to the USA in 1991. She has a long history of social activism dating back to the civil rights period and was active in the Gay Liberation Front. Now retired she pours her energies into trans activism and writing. Dawn is an incurable romantic, identifies as lesbian, and calls Philadelphia home. She lives in an attic apartment with several thousand books, a guitar, a mandolin and two elderly cats. She is grateful to Italy for having given the world gelato and to the Big Bang for having given us Planet Earth. She has a wicked sense of humor and doesn't take herself too seriously.

FAN PAGE

John McFarland

Once again I had fallen hook, line and sinker for one of Charles Loesser's very convincing lines. "We'll stay at The Drake, Jimmy. Chicago has some of the finest eateries in America. And don't forget the Art Institute, you'll love that. Plus the Symphony, if they're performing, would be fun," he said. I believed him without question that the trip would be a romantic getaway just as he promised, a way of getting back to what we'd recently been missing.

As it turned out, I was more like a companion/assistant responsible for keeping pests at bay during Charles's book-signing and publicity pit stops. It wasn't romantic; it wasn't a getaway; and, to add insult to injury, my sliver of a single room was down the corridor from his suite and next to the ice machine.

Now, I was sitting in the Drake's lobby, waiting for him to come downstairs after his nap. He had said six-thirty sharp, but he was late. When he finally did show up he seemed distracted. He didn't say "Hello," or "You look nice." The first thing out of his mouth was, "You are keeping a detailed record of everywhere we go, aren't you?"

He said, "When I hand the expenses to the accounting people I want them to understand that *everything* involved promotion for the new book."

I pulled out the hotel memo pad that I'd been using. I read, "Friday, 8:15 p.m., taxi from hotel (The Drake) to restaurant (The Place), arrive at 8:20; meeting with Ted Strozak (regional sales representative) for dinner and discussion of scheduled promotional activities . . ."

"Is that kind of detail noted for all entries, or just Friday's?" he asked, interrupting me.

"More or less," I said. "But you have the receipts and so . . ."

"Good," he said. "Just keep it up."

"Charles," I said, "is there something wrong?"

"No," he snapped.

I glared at him. "O.K., be that way."

He came around in a few moments and said, "I think that having a nap did me more harm than good. I'm in a much worse mood now than I was before."

"You should have come for a stroll with me. The streets are alive."

He ignored my remarks and said, "We better get going."

"How should I describe this next leg?" I asked.

He had left a voice mail on my room phone saying to "dress casually" so I had taken off my tie and replaced my sports jacket with a sweater vest. Dressed to the teeth, he looked like one of those supremely elegant, mature Yves St. Laurent models.

"Dinner with the Chicago-area group of fans," he said.

"*Really*?" I said. "A fan club?"

Now he glared at me. The nap *had* been a waste.

"Is that so far-fetched? I have an army of fans, you know."

"I meant," I explained in my most even-tempered manner, "an organized fan club, Charles. Of course, I know you have a huge number of fans. I'm one of them. You're a star."

At last he lowered himself into a chair beside me. Chagrin did not sit well on him.

"Jimmy, I apologize. I misunderstood your question." He ran his hand through his hair. He slouched down in the chair. "I'm a little anxious about this dinner."

"We could cancel," I said. "I saw a poster for the Symphony. They're doing a Delius."

He sat bolt-upright. "They can't perform English music," he said sharply. "Besides, we couldn't not show up."

That settled that.

"You've met this group before?" I asked.

"Not in the flesh," he said.

"How many people?" I asked

"Probably fifteen or so," he said. He was fidgeting. He wouldn't meet my eyes.

"And where are meeting them?"

"His house."

"Whose house?"

He reached into his jacket pocket and pulled out a slip of paper. He consulted it.

"Actually it's an apartment," he said.

"Private?"

"Very."

He was getting worse by the minute. What would happen by the time we got to the dinner? Would he be communicating in grunts?

"We need a back-up plan," I said.

He turned to face me and leaned forward, with his eyes lighting up.

"Brilliant," he said. "That's it exactly."

"If it gets bad, I get on my phone to check messages and then pretend we have an emergency summons to leave pronto."

He pushed himself out of the chair with vigor.

"Great!" he said. "I feel better already. You're better than a nap."

"See?" I said.

He motioned for me to get up. "One other thing. This Frederick claims to be a gourmet cook of some refinement, so if you have any food allergies, tell him at the start."

"Charles," I said as I stood up, "how did you get hooked up with this guy?"

"Fan mail," he said. "And then he wrote when he saw I'd be in Chicago and suggested this get-together with other local fans. . . . I must have been out of my mind to say yes."

"It could be fun," I said. "He's got good taste in books, after all."

Charles stepped up close to me. It seemed to take enormous effort on his part to spit out his next words. "But, Jimmy, some of my most dedicated fans are crazy. I don't mean zany, I mean clinically. And when I was waking up from my nap I started wondering if Frederick might turn out to be one of the nuttiest. We *are* in the general vicinity that was home to John Wayne Gacy and Jeffrey Dahmer. They were both fans of mine. You knew that, didn't you?"

"You're kidding," I said. I smiled.

"Would anybody claim them as fans if they weren't? I have the most darling letters from them both before and after their 'fame' and incarceration."

"God."

"That's what I mean. They *sound* completely reasonable at the start. Then you find out."

"I see why you wanted me along."

"That wasn't it," he said. "I thought this would be fun for us . . . you know, to be together . . . and I . . ."

"Charles," I said, "look, we have the fall-back plan. When you first sense trouble, you give me the signal and I go into action."

"Right, troops," he said, "now take a deep breath, hope for the best and on into the breach."

"O.K.," I said, "let's hop in a cab and go."

The cab ride was endless. We saw many, many flat, uninteresting streets in neighborhoods that went on forever before we arrived at the three-story brick courtyard building with large clapboard houses on either side of it.

Charles asked the cabbie if the last main street we'd been on was the best place to catch a cab for our return.

The cabbie said, "Listen, Mac, if you need a ride back, call forty-five minutes beforehand. This is the boonies. Nobody cruises for fares out here."

We paid up and climbed out. The cabbie tore off before we'd turned around.

"Does the reputation of the fan club precede them?" Charles asked. "What have we gotten ourselves into?"

"In forty-five minutes, they could broil us and be half-way to the bone," I said.

"He told me he lived close to downtown," Charles said.

"His first lie. Did he also claim to be hung and handsome?"

For the first time all day, Charles laughed.

"First sign of drool I see coming out of anyone's mouth, we put the fall-back plan in motion," he said. "Business shouldn't be murder."

"Torture is *our business*," I said. "They must be made to understand this."

We sauntered into the courtyard and rang the bell for the apartment. Buzzed in without having to identify ourselves, we hiked up the carpeted staircase. On the second floor landing, a very good-looking forty-ish man was waiting for us.

"Mr. Loesser?" he asked. "I'm Fritz Mendel. Welcome!"

Charles shook his hand.

I said, "I'm Jimmy Holden, Mr. Loesser's assistant," and extended my hand.

Fritz shook my hand vigorously while running his eyes from the top of my head to the tips of my toes. It was the royal welcome.

"Very pleased to meet you, Jimmy," he said. "Almost everyone has arrived. Your timing is perfect."

"The cab ride took forever," Charles said.

"It did?" Fritz said.

He was closing the apartment door behind us. We stood in the foyer and I watched to see if he shot a number of bolts closed on the door.

"Yes," said Charles.

"That's odd," Fritz said. "And you came directly from the hotel?"

"Yes," Charles said.

"It's only a twenty block ride," Fritz said. "You should have been here in ten minutes."

Charles and I looked at each other. All we could do was laugh.

"Oh," Fritz said, "you got a cabbie of the *old* school: fleece 'em and drop 'em. Welcome to the Big City!"

"Do we look like such rubes?" Charles asked.

"Let's get you both a drink," Fritz said and led us toward the living room.

It was a large rectangular space with hardwood floors and a high ceiling. The lights were low. Five or six people were sitting around, drinking and talking. There were no loose bones, hanks of hair or unusual devices with sharp spikes in sight.

Fritz announced, "We'll do introductions as soon as I get our guests of honor taken care of."

There was a great deal of nodding, but an atmosphere of sheer reverence prevailed. Everyone else looked ready for a cotillion. I was the most underdressed person in the room. I decided to get very drunk.

After we had our drinks in hand, Fritz walked us around the room and made introductions. The other guests had normal names like Carol, Leslie, Harris. Nobody looked insane. Of course, they never do, do they, until you find the bodies.

Charles loosened up more and more as each person told him how much his books meant to them and praised one or another by name with specific details. They *were* fans, not celebrity chasers. They could not have cared less about me, a mere appendage, but they had the good manners to ask how I liked being Charles's assistant. Since the whole story was a *lie*, I was free to make up anything at all or use a standard reply of "that was before my time."

To honor my pledge to get very drunk, I ambled back to the drinks table. Fritz, who hadn't yet exhibited any sociopathic red flags, was puttering around replenishing ice and glasses.

"How did the book-signing go?" he asked as he made me another Manhattan.

"Very well," I said. "There was a huge turn-out. Charles had to have his pen replaced three times."

"I *hate* that store," Fritz said. "They do get the traffic, no question about that, though. What can you do?"

"Marketing," I said.

I took the fresh drink from his hand.

"Packaging," he said and looked down at my crotch. He smiled. He was dazzling and as congenial a host as one could ask for.

"And how did you discover Charles's work?" I asked.

"Serendipity," Fritz said, "as with everything of lasting value."

"Do you think so?" I said.

"I do, indeed," he said and moved closer.

He traced a finger over the fine hairs on the index finger of the hand with which I held the glass. An electric sensation went through my body. I managed not drop the glass and bark like a dog. I smiled and took a sip of my drink.

"This is a very good Manhattan," I said.

"It's one of my satanic specialties," he said.

He was coming on to me and bringing up Satanism. That was more than enough for me, I didn't need to see foam pouring out of mouths before making my executive decision. I excused myself to make a faux-call, and we were out of there in five minutes flat.

In the cab ride back to The Drake, Charles said, "Though I was having a ball, to think I was edging *that* close to curtains! Imagine what a field day the media would have with that kind of exit for some-one like me. God, Jimmy, thank you, thank you and thank you."

I kept my mouth shut. It was the best choice.

John McFarland has published short fiction, criticism and essays everywhere from The BadBoy Book of Erotic Poetry *to* Cricket Magazine, *as well as in the anthologies* Charmed Lives: Gay Spirit in Storytelling *and* The Isherwood Century: Essays on the Life and Work of Christopher Isherwood. *He has also contributed biographical entries of glbtq.com, "the world's largest encyclopedia of gay, lesbian, bisexual, transgender, and queer culture."*

THE GREEN BENCH

Richard May

He was alone that morning, which disturbed me. Every day I walked through the park on my way to work and every day they were there, two old gentlemen, sitting on the green bench side by side, sleeves touching, if not arms. In winter they wore overcoats, in spring windbreakers maybe, in summer short sleeved shirts and in autumn something heavier, a regular coat probably.

Today, it was just him, the One on the Left. He was slumping but that wasn't unusual. He was quiet but that wasn't out of place either. I hardly ever saw them speaking to one another. They just sat, wordless, motionless, but together.

I had never had the urge to stop, to know their names, but today, with the One on the Right missing, I felt the need to know why. Where was he? I looked at my phone; I would be late. I never gave myself more than the minimum amount of time to make the transit from home to office. A brisk walk was good for you anyway. I sent a text to my secretary. I'd bring her coffee; she'd love me for it.

"Excuse me. You don't know me but I was wondering, where's your friend?" No, I can't say that. Much too personal. Besides, is the One on the Right a friend or a lover? A brother? They do tend to dress something alike.

"Pardon me but my name is Paul Stallings and…." No, that won't do either.

"Excuse me. Is this seat taken?"

"No," the One on the Left said, looking up with sad eyes in a sadder face. He moved towards the left end of the bench. I sat near the right. There was still space for the One on the Right in between us. I hoped he was coming. I really hoped he was coming.

We were silent together, like they were. But silence wouldn't answer my questions.

"Lovely day."

"Yes," he answered, looking up and around. I looked where he looked. We wound up looking at each other.

"Would you like the *Times*?"

"No," he answered, trying to smile. "We…I have it at home." His face fell. He turned away from me, perhaps to hide his sudden emotion, perhaps to keep it private.

I hesitated. "Is anything wrong? Can I help you?"

He turned back to me. "I wish you could."

That seemed like an invitation to intimacy so I moved closer, filling half the space we had left for the One on the Right. The One on the Left did not shift onto the other half.

"My name is Paul Stallings," I said, extending my hand.

He stared at it as if he were unfamiliar with the custom of shaking hands but then, belatedly and in a rush, grabbed for it like he was drowning. "My name is Clayton Evers." We shook and then held hands as seconds ticked. Mr. Evers' hand was calloused and strong. If I'd only shaken hands with him, without seeing his face and body, I would have guessed he was much younger. When he let me go, I felt regretful.

He visibly pulled himself together, sitting up straight, straighter than I'd seen him sit in three years of daily encounters, Monday through Friday only. "You're very kind," he said. I smiled. He took a breath.

"My partner died last night." That was as much as he could say. It seemed like a summary of much more.

I took his hand again and kept it. "I'm so so sorry. It seems awfully sudden."

"It was," he agreed, then pulled his hand out of mine, looking at me quizzically or suspiciously, I couldn't tell.

"I pass by here every day."

His expression remained wary.

"On my way to work."

He remained silent, leaning away from me, evaluating.

"I see you here every day when I pass."

He examined me more carefully, then seemed to relax. "Oh, yes. You're the Man Who Stares."

"What?"

"Bob and I noticed you always stare at us as you walk by. We called you the Man Who Stares. I'm sorry." He seemed embarrassed.

I tried to laugh, for his benefit. "I guess I did. I guess I was curious about the two of you. I mean, you're here every morning on the same bench, sitting beside each other, not saying anything."

Mr. Evers chuckled. "Well, we did talk *sometimes* I'm sure but, after 43 years, you don't need a lot of words."

We sat silently on the green bench for a few moments. Mr. Evers looked at the duck pond. I looked at nothing. I began to think I should be saying goodbye.

"Bob was 81, eight years older than I."

I liked the attention to grammar. I hesitated but then took the plunge. "Mr. Evers, pardon me, but could I ask how your partner died?"

"Of course. And my name is Clay." I nodded. He sighed and said in a shaky voice, "It was a heart attack. He'd had two before but recovered. This time...." His voice trailed off. I moved close beside him and put my arm around his shoulder. He leaned a little towards me. He probably did that with Bob.

"I'm sorry," he said. I could hear that he was crying very quietly. I held him more tightly.

"There is nothing to be sorry about."

"Oh, but there is. In 43 years you have plenty to be sorry about." His voice was rueful.

"But you were together all those years. You were in love." I was proud of myself for not stumbling over the word.

"Have you ever been in love?" he asked, looking askance at me but not pulling away. I shook my head no. "Well, I hope you find someone soon but when you do you'll know what I'm saying."

"I can't see myself 43 years with anybody."

"Why not?" he asked, turning in my arm to look more directly at me.

Why had I made it about me? Jack said I always did that. I disagreed with him when he said it, mainly because he was moving out and I was angry, but he was probably right. Looking back, he was right about most things we argued over.

"Oh, it's nothing."

"No, obviously it *is* something."

I could see he was interested. He must be a kind man. Maybe it would help…no, no, no! "I'm just being silly. It must be terrible for you right now."

"I'm afraid it's going to be terrible forever," he said, trying to make a joke out of it. He looked at me again and caught me checking the time. "I'm keeping you."

He was. I needed to go on, walk away, be at work. It was Friday. So much to do. "Are you going to be here tomorrow?" I asked him. He didn't look surprised, just said he would be. "I'll meet you here. What's a good time?" I wondered when he and Bob came to the green bench, when they left.

"We…." He stopped himself. "7:30 would be good."

"Okay, 7:30. See you then. Shall I bring you a coffee?"

"No, thanks. We always have…uh, yes. That would be great." I started to ask but he answered before I could. "Regular, one sugar please."

"Got it." I stood up and Clay stood with me. We shook hands again. "See you tomorrow," I promised.

"See you tomorrow," he agreed.

The next morning I made my way to the green bench carefully carrying his regular and my black coffee. I let out my breath when I saw him sitting there, in his usual spot.

"Good morning," I said to his back to let him know I was coming. He turned around, left arm resting along the back of the bench.

"Good morning, Paul." He had a lovely smile and a good profile. When I sat down beside him, I realized he was a very good looking man for his age. He must have been handsome when he was younger. What did—what had Bob looked like? Was he was handsome too? I'd really never seen his face.

"How are you doing today?" It was a pro forma ask but I really did want to know, once I'd said it.

"It's hard."

"Of course it is." I opened his coffee for him. He took several sips. "When is the funeral? You must have so much to do."

"Tomorrow. And no, I don't. Andrew, Bob's son, is taking care of everything, at least all that's left to take care of. Bob had already arranged most of it. He was a very organized person."

I tried to picture Bob. Clay seemed to be doing the same thing.

"Would you like to see a photo of him?" he asked. I said I would.

He took two out of his wallet. The first was of an elderly man with a wide smile and happy eyes. The second was of two men about my age, younger versions of Clay and Bob I could tell. Clay was indeed very handsome, very blond, with regular features and a thick moustache. Bob was not so attractive but he already had that wide smile and those happy eyes. He looked a little like me. I wondered if I should mention that to Clay.

"He had a great smile."

"He did," Clay said quietly. We stared at the photos for a while. I was beginning to get used to the silences. Clay looked up as if an idea had just occurred to him. "Would you come to his funeral?"

When I walked into Gershon's, the room was a sea of black suits and grey hair, with islands of blonde and brown. An usher handed me a program for the service. I hesitated, wondering where to sit, when suddenly Clay was in front of me, taking my forearm, welcoming me with words and smiles and guiding me towards the front. He introduced me to Bob's children and then sat us down.

"I saved a place for you."

I should have said, "You shouldn't have," and retreated towards the anonymous back of the room, but I didn't.

"Thank you."

He linked his arm comfortably through mine. I saw that Polly, Bob's daughter, noticed. I wondered what I should do but then the rabbi began and we all faced forward. I hadn't known Bob was Jewish too.

After the rabbi finished, quite a lot of friends and family rose to tell stories about Bob. I felt I got to know him, know why Clay stayed with him for over 40 years. When Clay tried to speak, he broke down almost immediately. Polly was beside him in a second, taking his arm, whispering. Andrew and I sat marooned on the bench, separated by the spaces where they'd been.

Afterwards, Polly spoke to me. "Thank you for coming."

"I'm Paul Stallings. I'm…."

"The Man Who Stares." She suppressed a smile. "Clay told us." She looked at me in an evaluating way. "You do look a lot like my father," she decided, as if she were confirming information given to her by another source. "I heard you saying the Kaddish. Are you Jewish?"

Clay joined us before I could answer. "Thank you so much for coming, Paul," he said, taking my hands in his. "Would you like to join us for lunch?"

I made some excuse.

"Will I see you tomorrow at the green bench?" he asked in a voice full of hope and dread. Polly's eyes gave their approval. Something inside me did too.

"Of course," I assured him. "I'll bring the coffee."

Richard May writes gay short stories, erotic and not. His work has appeared in several literary journals, short story anthologies and his first book Ginger Snaps: Photos & Stories of Redheaded Queer People. *Rick also organizes literary readings and events, including the annual Word Week literary festival, Noe Valley Authors Festival and Magnet San Francisco author events. He lives in San Francisco.*

UNCLE BILL

Gary Pedler

The restaurant looked like it was shot in black and white. White tablecloth and napkins on the table where Alan sat, a white candle, white carnations in a vase. Black walls and floor, black uniforms on the waiters. What little color there was, the dim lighting drained away. This look was fitting, since the person Alan was waiting for was someone out of the past, from the world of his childhood and before, memorialized in black and white photographs in his family's albums.

Alan went over in his mind some of the things he wanted to find out from Eddie. One question loomed large. "You've got to ask him," Alan told himself. "You'll kick yourself later if you don't."

Alan kept his eye on the entrance. It wasn't enough to look for a man in his sixties since that fit the description of much of the restaurant's clientele. He'd chosen this place on Polk Street because it was near where Eddie lived, but this wasn't a neighborhood he would have come to ordinarily. Polk Street had been the center of San Francisco's gay life in the sixties and early seventies, until Castro Street had elbowed it aside in the last four or five years. For Alan, at twenty-three, Castro Street was the gay present, vibrant, raucous, open, while Polk Street was the dreary, closeted past, where, after a furtive look around, one slunk into a bar with windows, if any, tinted so dark as to make the people within invisible.

Alan had only one photograph to help him identify Eddie, and that had been taken twenty years ago, at a Thanksgiving dinner. It showed Eddie seated at a table between Alan's mother, who was smiling, and his father, who was not. Eddie was short and slight, what looked like the bulge of a cigarette pack in the front pocket of his shirt. He gazed across the table through black-framed glasses, talking with someone on the other side. He sat forward in his chair and seemed a little taut, exerting himself to be agreeable. Bill had taken the photograph, Alan's mother, Fay, had explained, saying he wanted a picture of Eddie with the family. Later, Bill must have given the Hanstedts a copy.

A man came through the door who looked like an older version of the one in the photograph. Still short, still thin, still nervous-looking, still wearing glasses that didn't seem so much to help him see the world as make it harder for the world to see him. Clearly, Eddie had never been especially good-looking, but his compensation was to be one of those people whose appearance hadn't changed much over the years.

Alan stood up and raised his hand, catching the man's eye. "Eddie?" he said questioningly as the man approached.

"Yes." Eddie froze in front of Alan, staring at him, like a frightened animal.

"I'm Alan." Alan extended a hand, which Eddie shook after a moment's hesitation. "It's nice to meet you." Eddie said nothing. They both sat down. "You live not too far away, isn't that right?" Alan said.

"Yeah," Eddie said without expanding on this.

"Kay said you were staying in some sort of retirement home." It had been his Aunt Kay he'd asked for Eddie's telephone number. She'd sent Alan a piece of paper with only the name and number, as if to convey, I have nothing to say about your idea of contacting Eddie, and I don't want to know what happens if you do.

Again, "Yeah." Eddie's eyes slid from Alan to his two-toned surroundings.

A waiter came to their table. He was in his late thirties, young enough to strike a chord of desire in the middle-aged patrons, but old enough not to seem impossibly remote from their world. "What can I get you gentlemen to drink?"

"Nothing for me, thanks," Alan said. "Eddie, would you like something?"

"I'll have a gin and tonic."

Good, thought Alan. Maybe that will loosen him up.

In fact, the mere anticipation of the drink's arrival appeared to have this effect. "I live in the Dumbarton," Eddie said, "a residential hotel. I've got a nice big room on the fifth floor. There's a rec room with a piano, an organ, a pool table. We have Happy Hour there on Fridays and bingo on Tuesdays. I'm crazy about bingo. I go to all the different games in the city. You can play bingo somewhere every day if you want. I used to earn all my spending money from bingo. I haven't been so lucky lately."

Once Eddie started talking, it was as if he couldn't stop. "The one thing I don't like is having to pay sixty-five dollars every month for meals, even though I haven't set foot in the dining room for over a year. The food is terrible; they keep it warm for hours on those steam trays. Someone told me there's a law in front of Congress to stop them making you pay for food in a place like that. They say it should be illegal to try to force people to eat something. Anyway, I usually get take-out food and bring it up to my room. We're not supposed to, but the clerks turn a blind eye."

"Well, I want you to have a really nice meal this evening," Alan said as Eddie's drink arrived. "It's my treat, remember." Normally at his age, he would have expected the older man to pay; but Eddie, with his rumpled clothes and thinning hair, was like some lonely old man he'd found sitting on a park bench and wanted to help in some way.

Eddie took a substantial sip from his glass. "I think I'll have the steak. I haven't had a decent steak in a long time."

A week ago when Alan had telephoned him, Eddie had seemed uneasy, almost suspicious. Alan had introduced himself and said he understood Eddie had known his uncle, Bill Hanstedt. Yes, Eddie said, he'd been a friend of Bill's. "Friend," Alan noted to himself. Alan explained he was taking an interest in his family history and wanted to learn more about Bill, whom he'd never met. "I'm not sure what I can tell you," Eddie said. Alan wondered for a moment if he had the story wrong. But no, that couldn't be, he'd talked to too many people in the family.

After they'd given the waiter their orders, Alan took up the thread. "So you knew my Uncle Bill?"

"I did." At the mention of this name, Eddie became quiet again. Alan tried a more specific question.

"What was Bill like?"

Eddie's gazed into his glass. "The main thing about Bill was that everyone liked him."

Alan imagined Ryan, his father, materializing beside him to add his own views. "Bill could be charming when he wanted," Ryan said, "obnoxious when he wanted."

His mother wouldn't want to be left out of the discussion, Alan was sure. A figmentary Fay looked about her with eyes in which a girlish earnestness had persisted down the years.

"I always had the feeling Bill was keeping his distance," she said. "He was friendly enough, but a little aloof."

"He was a serious person," his father said. "Well, he had reason to be. He had a pretty hard life. Harder than mine, at any rate." Ryan narrowed his shrewd blue eyes. "When we were young, I hated Bill. We fought all the time."

A phantom of his Aunt Kay joined the group, sitting down heavily across from Alan. Kay was ten years older than Ryan, a half-sister of his and Bill's from a previous marriage of their mother's. Kay was short and stout, her braided white hair wound into a crown atop her head. "I remember Al running through the house, just a little guy, shouting, 'I'm going to kill him! I'm going to kill him!' He sounded like he meant it."

"Bill was a couple of years older than your father," Fay said, "and his parents sent him to the same high school. Teachers would ask if he was Bill Hanstedt's brother. 'Bill was such a good student,' they'd say, 'and I hope you will be, too.' Ryan dreaded that."

Photographs scattered themselves across the table. Bill at six or seven standing between two rose bushes, with plump cheeks and a round bell-shaped hat, a little pensive, hands behind his back. At a rustic cabin in Yosemite, a teenage Bill with shiny dark hair and Ryan, still tow-headed, at opposite ends of the long porch; Kay and their mother sitting in between, as if the two boys needed to be kept apart. Bill in his cap and gown before his high school graduation, arms held stiffly at his side.

Fay spoke. "Mrs. Hanstedt told me that in the year after high school, Bill just sat in his room all day. He even took his meals up there."

"Bill had the top floor of the house all to himself," Kay said. "You could see the ocean from the window on a clear day."

Alan had made a trip out to the Richmond District to see the house on Tenth Avenue. Gazing up at the third floor window, he'd pictured Bill looking out. "What was he doing up there all that time?" Alan questioned.

None of the others could say.

Dora, Kay's oldest daughter, drifted around the table, as if unsure how much she had to contribute to the talk. "After my parents divorced, my mother moved back into the Hanstedt home with me. My mother told me to give Uncle Bill a wide berth. He was in a deep funk, or unwell, I don't know which. He ignored me, and I pretty much ignored him. The family's attitude was, Poor Bill. Then all of a sudden, he started living again."

"How do you mean?" Alan asked. "What happened?" But Dora only made a gesture of uncertainty, continuing her drift.

"I had the impression he didn't like children," Dora went on. "Imagine my surprise when he went to San Francisco State and got a teaching credential."

Kay wiped her eyes with a crumpled tissue; she had some problem that made them water. "Jobs were hard to come by in the Depression, especially teaching positions. The only one Bill could find was at a lumber camp outside of McCloud. He taught the children of all the lumbermen, first grade to ninth."

A pile of letters from Bill appeared on the table, given to Alan by his Aunt Kay. He'd expected these to be a treasure trove—actual letters from his mysterious Uncle Bill. In fact, they were rather pedestrian. Descriptions of the cabin he lived in, accounts of the cold in winter, requests to have more of his clothes mailed to him, thanks for the box of cookies Kay had sent. There didn't even seem to be any lines that Alan could read between. The few interesting details came instead from family members, that Bill had eaten his meals with the lumbermen, that there had been talk of his marrying the woman who was superintendent of schools in the county. "Our mother was against the marriage," Kay said. "Maybe by then she had some idea. . . ."

"Bill was pretty isolated up there," Alan's father said. "He got involved with a ham radio club. To be admitted, he had to join the naval reserves. That meant he was called up as soon as the war started. Later, he applied to become an officer. He got his commission while he was at sea, so the other officers chipped in with pieces of the uniform. I joined the Navy, too." He added with a sour face, "As usual, my brother outranked me."

Another photograph dropped onto the table, Bill in his officer's uniform. Arms folded, confident smile, eyes gazing into the distance. Under his officer's cap, his hair had turned gray in his early thirties, like Ryan's. He also shared with his brother a not very shapely nose, as he did with Alan. Kay gave the picture an admiring look. "The photographer put a copy of this in his store window as an advertisement for his work. He must have thought people would like it."

"At the end of the war," Ryan said, "when the guy discharging me asked if I was sure I wanted to leave the Navy, I hardly gave him time to finish his question before I said, 'Yes!' Bill got out, too, but not without a good long think. He was an officer by then and had a lot of friends in the service."

"Bill was so handsome," Fay said, studying the photograph. "I wondered why some gal didn't snag him."

Ryan raised his eyebrows. "You did your best to set him up with your sister."

"I did no such thing!" Fay turned to Alan. "When your father and I got married, Bill gave us a wedding present, naturally. I had an idea Bill would never get married himself, so when he moved to that apartment on Webster Street, I gave him a pressure cooker as a house-warming present instead."

An old address book of his mother's materialized, open to "H." Several addresses for Bill were crossed out as he moved ever farther from the city center, from the cells of worker-bees encrusting the slopes of Nob Hill to the leafier, less intensely urban outer districts. Alan, who lived near Bush and Powell, where the *tang tang* of the cable car was scattered across his days, wondered if he would follow the same trajectory.

Eddie had been working steadily away at his steak, making little noises of pleasure. Well-done at his request, it looked nearly black in the low light, while Alan's chicken breast was so pale it was almost white. "I was so eager to get out of Montana when I was a kid," he said at last. "I'd stand outside the vaudeville house in our town and beg the players to take me away to Chicago, New York. But you know, there must still be a little of the Montana boy in me, because I sure do love a good steak."

Kay turned her watering eyes on Eddie. "Bill was living with Eddie by that time."

"Eddie," Ryan said, pursing his mouth. "He was so different from anyone else Bill ran with."

"Bill was good-looking," Dora said, "and had good-looking friends, male and female. Eddie was not good-looking."

"A stock clerk at Roos-Atkins," Kay sniffed.

Fay gazed at Eddie with wide eyes. "Eddie didn't have many friends, as I recall. I had the impression Bill was his main connection to the world."

Dora shrugged. "I suppose Bill's attitude was, Poor Eddie, he needs looking after."

Fay ran a finger thoughtfully over her chin. "'Maybe they're just friends,' I said to myself. 'But maybe they're something else.'" She turned to Ryan. "But I never said anything to you, and you never said anything to me. I didn't want to embarrass you."

"Yes," Eddie murmured through a bite of steak, "everyone liked Bill. I remember when he taught at San Quentin—you know about that, don't you, his teaching there after the war?" Alan nodded. "One prisoner would wait by the window of his cell for Bill to walk past. He called him Mr. Hansty; he never got the name right. He would stand there, waiting, just to say hello, hoping Bill would talk to him for a bit."

Eddie finished first his steak, then a second drink. "Something else about Bill, he was very well-educated. He read all the time. Maybe you're like that, too; you said you work in a library. Bill never put other people down, though. Never used a fifty-cent word and made you feel stupid. Now me, I'm not well-educated. People always told me that was what was holding me back." Eddie gave a shake to his glass, as if hoping to loosen a little more gin and tonic from the ice cubes. "Anyway, Bill was just an all-round great guy. We didn't have a single argument the whole time we knew each other."

Alan buttered a piece of bread, not particularly wanting to eat it, more to have something to do while he ventured, "I hope you don't mind my asking, but—was Bill gay? I am, so I've always been curious."

"Yeah, Bill was gay." Eddie didn't admit that he himself was, Alan noticed. "That prisoner I was telling you about, he was gay, too. But he wouldn't keep a low profile and was always getting into trouble. Bill went to bat for him many times. Of course, the man didn't know Bill was gay. No one at the prison did."

"My brother never told me he was a homosexual," Ryan said, "but then he never told me anything of importance."

"You could see something was troubling Mrs. Hanstedt," Fay said. "There was something no one in the family mentioned, some skeleton in the closet. It's much better nowadays, when people can discuss these things."

"How did you two meet?" Alan asked Eddie.

"Sunbathing in Lafayette Park," he said, "in that flat part at the top." Alan knew the spot. Thirty years on, it was still a place to sunbathe, ringed by trees that provided shelter from the wind, and still a cruisy area. "We lived together for fifteen years, first on Webster Street, then Fulton. After that, we bought the house on Belvedere."

The house on Belvedere; Alan had already heard about this. Belvedere was an almost-island, a wooded ridge out in the Bay linked to the rest of Marin by a causeway. He asked Eddie how they'd found the house. Eddie said they were visiting a friend next door, a gay friend, and the for-sale sign had just gone up.

"'What do you think?' Bill said to me. 'Shall we buy it?' I said yes. The house cost nineteen thousand back then. A friend told me it sold for two hundred and fifty not too long ago. It was on the 'preferred side' as the Islanders say, the one that isn't as windy. The Two Boys in Belvedere, people called us."

Not owning a car, Alan had never bothered to get out to the house, but he had an idea what it looked like from his mother. It had been built to resemble a log cabin, a style that had had a short vogue. A big stone fireplace, a view of the water through the pines.

"I'd get off from my job at Roos-Atkins and take the bus home," Eddie reminisced. "Bill was working at an elementary school in

Novato by then, and he got off at three. He was always there at the bottom of the hill to meet me, either on foot or with the car. We'd go places on the weekends. We had a lot of nice friends, high-class people, doctors, lawyers, artists. We went to a lot of nice parties."

"It was brave of you to live together back then," Alan said. He was going through a period of reading books with titles like *Out of the Closets and into the Streets*. He was convinced sweeping social changes were taking place that made the present sharply different from the past and would render the future almost unrecognizable.

Eddie gave a shrug that suggested he didn't see things in quite the same way. "Once someone at the school talked about Bill living with another man, and it looked like trouble was brewing. But then that quieted down. As I said, everyone liked Bill, and he had such a good reputation among his fellow teachers. The thing to do was keep them separate, your private life and your work life. It's like having your salad on one plate and the main course on another."

"What did Bill's family think, though, and your family?"

"My family was way off in Montana and had other things on its mind, like making ends meet. As for Bill's parents, I'm sure it never occurred to them that Bill and I were that way."

"Bill brought Eddie to all the family gatherings," Ryan said, "at Thanksgiving, Christmas."

"My recollection is no one ever said anything about Eddie," Fay mused. "Not a word. They didn't say they liked him or didn't like him, or thought he was this or that. No criticism, no praise. Just nothing." Her eyes shifted to Alan. "I just want to say that I would have married your father even if I'd known about Bill and thought it might be something that ran in the family."

Eddie gave a snorty laugh. "It seemed silly for anyone to make a fuss about what Bill and I did in bed because we hardly did anything. Bill was a great guy, but I think he must have had a low sex drive."

Alan's mother directed a glance at his father that said, Something else may have run in the family.

"We visited your folks a couple of times," Eddie said to Alan. "Once we didn't even go in the house, just picked some fruit off your trees. You had fruit trees, didn't you?"

"Yes," Alan said absently, wondering, Did Bill and I meet on one of those visits, the two black sheep in the family? The Hanstedt family album appeared among the other material spread across the restaurant table, opened to black and white photographs of Alan playing dress up as a child. Alan was a Victorian Lady in broad-brimmed hat, carrying a broken umbrella that served as a parasol. A Fairy Princess in an old petticoat of his mother's, stepping forward demurely in white yarn slippers decorated with pompoms. His parents could dismiss this behavior as "just a phase." It was harder to imagine Bill doing so. Harder to imagine him not uncomfortable in any meetings he might have had with the budding sissy. Perhaps if they could have met when Alan was older, a teenager—but five years after Alan appeared on the scene, Bill made his exit.

"We'd come home from a party," Eddie said. "All Bill had to drink was one brandy, but he said he felt terrible and threw up on the floor in his bedroom. I asked if he wanted me to call a doctor. No, he said. Bill was always up before me, but he wasn't the next morning. I called out, 'Bill, how come you're not up yet?' I looked in his bedroom. He wasn't there. I tried to open the bathroom door, but couldn't, something was blocking it. I finally managed to get it open. Bill was lying there dead. He'd probably been there for a few hours, the doctor told me later. I kept going on about how if only I'd known, I could have gotten him to a hospital, but the doctor said he'd died at once. It was the worst kind of heart attack you can have, the kind where the heart just stops. I forget what they're called. There he was, lying on the floor, one arm over his face, like he was asleep."

Alan listened, looking down at the table, and so did his parents, Aunt Kay, and Dora, hovering behind Kay's chair.

"At the funeral, there were fifty or sixty bouquets," Eddie went on. "Lots of people. Fellow teachers, students, friends, family, Navy pals.

All the pallbearers were gay. Of course, in those days, you couldn't tell. A full military ceremony. You know how they fold the flag and hand it to the chief mourner? They gave it to me, not one of his relatives. I have an idea the undertaker was gay and arranged that. I still have that flag in a drawer."

A long silence. At last Fay said, "At the funeral, Eddie broke down, like the widow. My sister turned to me and said, 'Well, now we know for sure.'"

"I've never heard anyone carry on like that," Ryan said, faintly disapproving. "He cried and cried and cried, moaned and wailed. He had to have someone on either arm to support him while he walked."

"No one else shed a tear," Fay said, "only Eddie."

Ryan looked toward his half-sister. "Kay certainly didn't. I thought that was strange at the time. Later I found out she knew all about the will. Bill left everything to Eddie. Kay and Bill had been very close, but the will changed that. She's never said a good thing about him since."

Kay wiped her eyes with the tissue. "Bill was for Bill. Selfish."

"I asked her once if she still kept in touch with Eddie," Fay said. "'No,' she told me. That was all, just 'no.' I didn't either." Fay's gaze shifted toward Eddie, then, without quite reaching him, moved away again. "Sometimes I feel bad about that."

"Bill had a mean expression on his face," Eddie mused. "Like he was saying he didn't want to die. He'd been planning to retire early. He was only fifty." Eddie's eyes were fixed on the black wall behind Alan. "It was two years before I stopped crying every night, thinking about that man. We were such a good balance for each other. He had brains, charm, and I – well, I guess I had more common sense."

The waiter arrived with the check. Alan took charge of it, as promised, and Eddie made no attempt to stop him, as if he didn't even see it. "How long did you stay in the house?" Alan asked.

"Four years," Eddie said. "I tried renting out the other room, but that didn't work. The taxes kept going up. Eventually I sold it."

Amid the small movements that followed, the rising from the table, putting on coats, walking toward the door, the phantom figures disbursed. They had nothing more to say.

Alan and Eddie stepped outside into the cool cloudy night. Eddie asked, "What about you? Are you seeing anyone?"

"No," Alan said. He wanted to experience the automatic superiority of the young, but the fact was, Eddie had had fifteen years with Bill, and Alan's love life so far was full of vanishing tricks, like a magician's act.

"My advice is, don't," Eddie said.

"You got involved with Bill."

"I should have said, Unless you find someone special, like Bill. And I only found one of those."

They headed north along Polk Street. Without having discussed their destination, Alan was walking Eddie to his hotel on O'Farrell. "I have a friend now," Eddie said. "We don't have sex; it's just for the companionship. He's a very nice man. We travel a lot, to Reno, other places. Bill was never much for traveling."

"Just like my dad," Alan remarked.

"Oh look, this antique store has closed. Well, it was more like a junk shop anyway." Eddie peered through the window at the dark, empty interior. The window gave back a dim reflection of their figures standing in the street. Putting a hand to his face, Eddie said, "It's funny. When I look in the mirror, I say, 'Gosh, you look old.' I don't feel old, though. I'm sixty-seven, but I feel just the way I did at thirty-seven."

"You're lucky," Alan said.

"Here we are." Eddie stopped in front of the Dumbarton, a brick building like many others stacked together on the street. "It was nice meeting you. Bill's nephew." Eddie looked at Alan as if truly seeing him for the first time. Alan wondered if he was noticing family resemblances as he himself had earlier, studying the photographs. Possibly involving a not very distinguished nose.

"I hope we can meet again," Alan said, though aware only a single thread connected them. Eddie held out his hand. Alan took it in his for a moment – it was thin and cold – then let it go.

While Alan walked home, it started to rain. As he reached the bars and restaurants near Union Square, color seeped back into the world through the many neon signs, repeated on the wet sidewalks in softer forms.

Born and raised in Napa Valley, educated at UC Santa Cruz, and a resident of San Francisco for over two decades, Gary Pedler might have seemed destined to remain a Bay Area fixture. Yet after an escape from his role as a white-collar wage slave, he's been off seeing other parts of the world, traveling in Asia, the Middle East, and Europe, and of course drawing inspiration from his experiences. Gary has written two novels, two short story collections, a travel memoir, a YA novel, and, a little to his surprise, a play. More information about Gary and his work can be found at www.garypedler.com.

STOP THE CAR

Mark McNease

I t was a drug run, sure, but that doesn't change what we saw. One thing had nothing to do with the other, and had it not been real, had we not witnessed it with our own eyes and my intention was to convince people of what I knew to be untrue, I wouldn't mention that part of it at all! I'd say we had been coming back from band practice or a visit to my family. But it had been absolutely real, so I tell it without leaving out the detail that inevitably makes people think it was all a hallucination. It was not! I don't *care* if people say, well, of course you saw a spaceship, you were taking drugs, what else would you see? Angels, goblins, ghosts along the road hitching for a ride. Go ahead, dismiss us, I've said all these years. You don't have to believe me—and getting you to has never been the point. Telling what we saw and what happened to us, as if I were in a court of law having promised to tell the truth with my hand on a bible, that has been the only point.

Three nineteen-year-olds zipping down an Indiana back road in 1977, exceeding the speed limit as if someone were chasing us through the dark. Charlie and me in the back seat trying out the merchandise, Debs driving, her hands gripping the wheel so tightly her knuckles were white and her eyes button-wide in panic, imagining her next birthday in a jail cell. It had taken all we had to convince her to go. We couldn't take a bus, we said, the trip was too long, and all those stops! Who would take us seriously as entrepreneurs in the college drug trade if they knew we brought our supply in on a Greyhound? And besides, it would be less dangerous driving back late at night off the main highways—even cops were asleep that time of night and other cars were few and far between.

I think that's what they count on, these aliens, why they take their interstellar breaks on back roads and farm land—fewer witnesses. I mean, when has a starship ever stopped to admire the view over downtown Los Angeles, or hovered above the White House wondering what all the fuss was about? It's not us they want to see, any more than they want us to see them. We come in the billions, crawling around on the planet like so many ants. No, it's our real estate they covet, our vast expanses and plant life, our vistas, canyons and rolling hills. We're so much road kill to them, and if it weren't for the opportunity to study us like frogs pinned to a board in biology class, I doubt they would bother with us at all.

It's always out there on a country road where they can practice their crowd control, minimize their risks. We just happened to be there at the time. It doesn't matter that Charlie and I were wide awake on speed we planned to sell for twice our cost, or that we'd smoked our last joint to take the edge off once we'd exited the toll road. It's not like it was *acid*. And even if it had been, I'd never seen anything like that on a trip. It was absolutely tangible, absolutely something I will never forget—our car beneath a clear black sky dotted with a million stars, this giant *thing* floating in the sky so close you could hit it with a rock if you threw hard enough. Enormous and silent, so big we thought it was a building or a tower of some kind, until we realized there was nothing holding it up.

That's when we started shouting, "Stop the car! Stop the car!"

Granville, Indiana, isn't the center of anything but itself. It's got a couple rivers that wisely pass it by on two sides of town. It's got a couple malls that killed the downtown when I was still a kid riding my bike to grade school. It's got a water tower with the town's name on it—a name whose origin nobody seems to know. Maybe it was a man named Granville, some guy who started it all with a squatter's farm a hundred fifty years ago, or maybe it was some rich family from Chicago who built a second home there and everything else just grew up around it. Or maybe it just *happened*, the way some towns come to be. One person built a house, then somebody else built another nearby, and after so long the people living there gave it a name. I'll never know, and I'll never care. It's just the place I grew up and couldn't wait to leave two days after I got my high school diploma. I was meant for bigger things, like moving to Bloomington for a first-rate education at Indiana University, majoring in something I would decide later, once I had a better picture of my place in the universe. Marine biology, maybe—I'd kept an aquarium when I was a kid and lost fewer than half my fish to attrition. Or maybe comparative religion. They all seemed pretty whacky to me, and it might be fun to compare their idiosyncrasies. *Something* that would maintain my trajectory from small town loner to respected authority, a man whose knowledge and expertise outweighed the fact he had few friends. One of only a handful in the world who knew what I knew, and who could thus afford to be eccentric and reclusive. A Stephen Hawking or a Jacques Cousteau. It never occurred to me I'd have to work to get there, and that dropping out after two semesters was not the best career path. So I ended up living in a rented house with a guy named Charlie, selling speed to the kids who stayed the university course and needed it for all night study sessions. And that's as famous as I ever got—the go-to guy for Christmas trees and black beauties. The local dealer with a connection in Granville, of all places, making runs once a month to buy a supply from Janet Carlson's mother. Yes, that's right. Her mother, with her small town mob ties and her entire family engaged in a criminal enterprise. I forgot to say that—that I'd been a drinker in high school, a pill-popping pothead whose only friends in Granville were like me, kids who couldn't wait to get out, and in the meantime made our escape in a tablet or a joint that could be traced back to Janet's mother. Skinny, chatty, bug-eyed Janet, with her stringy hair and her palpable paranoia, chain smoking, jumping at any sound. The most popular girl in school if you were inclined to break the law.

I don't remember the exact night, or the month, or what season it was, although it hadn't been too cold. Memory fades that way, dissolving with brain cells as time erodes them away. I know I was living with Charlie, sleeping on a mattress on the floor. I know the roof leaked in the kitchen—it was a crappy little house off-campus the owner had never lived in, buying it on the cheap to rent to students. It didn't matter I was not one, or that Charlie had never been one. We paid the $200 a month in cash, and that was all the cranky old man who took it from us cared about. We didn't even know if he was the owner. He was just the unpleasant dwarf (he was very short, not really a dwarf, but we called him that) who showed up the first of every month to take the money and run.

We fancied ourselves outlaws, edge-livers, convinced we were known by the police, tracked in the vice squad files, so we kept our mouths shut about the leaking roof and the broken toilet tank and the holes in the walls where doorknobs banged against them. The less contact we had with anyone in authority the better. We were kingpins, a two-man cartel financed by the Granville mob. We slept three, maybe four nights a week, the rest of the time staying up till dawn answering phone calls, making deliveries, and generally restless from amphetamine psychosis.

Charlie was the only friend I had in Bloomington until Debs came along and made us a gang. He'd lived there all his life, a local boy who swam in the quarries as a kid and who viewed the college students with undisguised contempt, except when they were handing him fifty bucks for a bag of weed or a bottle of pills. I couldn't blame him, either. This was a way station for them, a place they came to prepare for success, while boys like Charlie got nowhere and stayed there. Semi-literate hoodlums whose fathers had failed before them, so they worked in gas stations or hamburger joints and they soothed their deflated egos in local bars where a fake ID was as good as any. The Charlies of the world were losers to them, but he had what they wanted and they both knew it, so over they came when the sun went down, and into the house they walked as if, for an hour, they were equals. Charlie made them stay that hour, too. He enjoyed that part of it, offering up a joint and getting us all to watch TV with the sound off. The kids with their majors in music or law would play along, becoming inarticulate, throwing out slang and double negatives like "ain't nobody" and "don't do no harm", peppered with "fuck" this and that, all of us, for that short while, in on a game outside polite society.

But I knew Charlie better. I knew him as the guy who wrote poetry in a spiral notebook, who watched public broadcasting and had a passion for archeology. The guy who couldn't bring himself to ask a girl out, so he settled for masturbation and a stack of magazines. The guy whose dreams were too big for Indiana, waiting for the right opportunity to leave it behind. We had that in common, fancying ourselves players in a larger scheme of things who just had to keep it going long enough for that one big break that would take us up and out of there.

And I loved the guy, truth be told. All that swimming had done wonders for his body, lithe and prepared for flight at the sound of a siren. His hair was long, and he would tie it back with a rubber band and let the tail flow down between his shoulders. His skin was pale—he spent little time in the sun, writing his poems and selling his drugs when most people were in for the night—and he had the smooth appearance of a young man who'd never known a blemish in his life. His eyes were the brown of light chocolate, and in them I could see everything from passion to indifference, depending on whether or not we had any witnesses. For Charlie maintained a studied detachment I understood completely: a method of survival for minimum-wage poets whose friends and fathers would not go easily on sons with dreams. Ambition was for suckers, fools and faggots. A love for classical music or poetry was a love to be hidden. But sometimes, around me, his loves came out, and I loved him for it, and I kept that hidden, too.

We met through his ad for a roommate. He'd already been living in the house for six months. His previous roommate, known only as "the asshole," had left owing Charlie two months' rent. Charlie never said his name, and I learned quickly enough not to pry. I would never know more about my predecessor than I knew about Charlie's family, and that was okay. What mattered was where we were, in that day, at that moment, not where we'd come from or who we'd left behind.

I have no idea why spaceships dock where the fewest people will see them. They have all this technology, all this power to come and go as they please across galaxies. Why would they care if ten people saw them, or a thousand? But that's the way it is, and that's the way it was that night as we drove along a two-lane road with our contraband and our hopes for a tidy profit.

Those little things in life that shock us are never expected. I mean, how pointless is it to say, when something extraordinary happens, "I never expected that!" *Of course* we never expected it—that's what makes it startling!

Charlie and I had nothing more significant on our minds that night than getting back to Bloomington, taking the jars of speed we had and breaking them down into 100-tab orders, bagging them up and calling our anxious customers. The only thing Debs had on her mind was making it back without a traffic stop that would land her in prison for the next twenty years. She wasn't like us. She didn't get high, she wanted to be a social worker and change the lives of a few dozen people over the course of her career. She'd been convinced for months that throwing her lot in with the likes of us was asking for trouble. A conspiracy theorist, she believed the government had long been keeping an eye on pretty much everyone. (A prescient girl, that Debs; though I have no idea where she is now—probably underpaid in some aid agency for the poor—I'm sure she's taken the whole Homeland Security thing as vindication of her paranoia.) She wasn't Charlie's girlfriend, or my best buddy, the way Fat Tina had been in high school when I first came to terms with my attraction to guys. Debs was a hanger-on, sharing an outsider status with us, but she had plans. Having her life derailed by a drug bust was not one of them.

We were probably halfway back—it's hard to tell how far we'd driven on long straight back roads in the dark, Charlie and I wide awake in the back seat but inattentive, Debs clutching the steering wheel and driving as fast as she could to get us home, but I'd say about halfway. We hadn't seen another car for a good twenty minutes, just the lights from an occasional house. The radio didn't work. Something clanged in the engine, ticking the time away. Charlie and I had started to come down, a most unpleasant set of sensations that always accompanied the tail end of a speed buzz. Grinding teeth, a pit in the stomach, irritability and a desire to go up or down, any direction that would take us out of the anxiety.

That was when I looked out the window and saw it. A large building, or at least the *top* of a large building. There were colored lights around a high floor, and for a moment I thought that was a strange choice of lighting, as odd as the location. Who the hell has a building in the middle of farmland, the center of nowhere? I leaned up with my face a few inches from the side window, wanting to take a closer look at the rest of it, the *bottom* of the building, where I expected to see a few people working late or a cleaning crew making its way floor to floor. That's when I realized there was no bottom. Okay, okay, I thought, it's not a building. It's a tower. A water tower, maybe, shaped

. . . not in a circle, as a tower would be, but a triangle. A big triangle in the sky. I stared harder, squinting, trying to focus, to see the tower's legs outlined against the night sky, not thinking how unlikely it was to have a massive lighted tower out here where it had no use. And that's when it hit me—there were no legs. It was not a building or a tower. It was a *thing*, still and silent in the sky, not hovering. Hovering implies movement, however slight, and this giant triangular colored-lighted goddamn thing was perfectly motionless a hundred or so feet above a field.

"Uh, Charlie, dude," I said, reaching over and poking his arm, not wanting to take my eyes off it, "Charlie, wake up."

"I'm not fucking asleep," he said. "How the fuck am I gonna sleep on this shit? It's cheap speed, man, we gotta find another source."

"Look," I said, ignoring his opinion. "Out there. Look!"

Charlie leaned over and put his face near mine, peering out the window.

"What the fuck is that?" he said, much quicker to pick up on its strangeness than I had been.

"A tower maybe," I said.

"A tower without legs?"

Much quicker indeed.

We both stared at it, taking in its shape and the lights that rimmed it, now pulsing, I realized. Not dozens, but just a few, like portals with the colors emanating outward—red and green and blue.

It came to us at the same time. This was a vehicle of some kind, suspended in the air. Big as a football field, so large we had barely passed it in the seemingly endless minutes it had taken us to give it our full attention. We knew what it was, fantastic as it seemed.

I bolted up, leaning my hand over the seat.

"Stop the car!" I said.

Debs did not take her eyes off the road ahead. I know she thought we'd slipped into psychosis. Speed freaks were susceptible to that—but we weren't speed freaks. We just sold it and tested the supply for quality. We weren't any more stoned than we ever were, and never had we hallucinated a spaceship or anything more pronounced than a few flashing lights and quivering sidewalks.

"Stop the car!" Charlie chimed in, instantly alert now, his eyes fixed on the great machine.

We must have frightened poor Debs. The more urgent our pleas, the more frozen her face became, the more rigid her grip on the steering wheel.

All I could think as we began to pull away from it, to leave it behind us, was what might happen if we pulled over and got out. What adventure might welcome us if we stepped out of the car, onto the side of the lonely dark road with no one near and nothing to distract us but that *thing* up in the sky.

I heard it then, my own voice in my head—or so I think, so I remember, not saying it out loud but feeling it with all the longing of a lost child who sees his home in the distance . . .

I want to go! I want to go!

Please take me.

I want to go.

Somebody heard me, up there.

It moved, this massive object that had been fixed the moment before. Something about it changed, the lights brightened, *it knew we were there.*

The car slowed, the engine died. My eyes grew heavy, I was not anxious anymore. Frozen in time, that's how it felt. Frozen and slipping rapidly into dreamless sleep, and the next thing I knew, I was gone.

We all remember the womb. We are our own eyewitnesses. It doesn't matter that we can't describe it—at the very beginning of ourselves we had no words. What we remember is deep within us, told in our reactions to sounds and smells, the positions we sleep in and the pull of the ocean, its great rocking motion so familiar.

It was in that place, *up there*, that I can try to describe, as I might describe the sound of voices heard from inside my mother. Recalling it as an experience, not a thing for which I have hard evidence; not a place I visited from which I brought back a rock or a scalpel. It's a memory, and memories lack substance. Memories cannot be taken from a pocket and given to anyone. Memories are stories to be told, which is all I'm attempting to do.

I was cold, but no more so than an October day. That was my first impression, as consciousness seeped back into me, a surrounding coolness that didn't come from a vent, didn't seem manufactured. As if the temperature of the place could be neither higher nor lower, set, as might be the surface of the moon or the center of an ice cube.

I was alone but not alone, so startled by the place it didn't occur to me where Charlie and Debs might be. In fact, I had forgotten them, and I wondered if the room around me was the interior of a lucid dream into which I had come awake. I'd had a lucid dream a time or two—those strange, marvelous experiences where you wake up in your dream, and you know you're dreaming. If you can stay awake long enough, there in your dream, a sense of power comes to you as you realize you can do anything, cross mountains of time by simply wanting to, or move yourself from one side of a cavern to the other just by thinking it.

Was I dreaming? Had the car crashed and left me in a coma, and this was where the comatose went?

I wondered these things for a moment only, as it became clear to me I was not dreaming. I could feel my body, freed from clothing, flesh pressed against a metal counter, if metal it could be called. My back hurt, and my arms were heavy as I lifted one, then the other, across my bare chest. I had no impulse to cover myself—it seemed completely natural to me to lie there exposed, as if I were home in bed. (What is nakedness, anyway, but something we're compelled to hide from others? And while there were others there—I could sense them looking at me—there was also no one.) The space around me began to take form, a large open area that didn't appear to have any corners. I suppose that's why it struck me less as a room than a place, an *area*, that had walls but no straight edges. The floor became the walls became the ceiling, a fluid, oval space more womblike as my eyes adjusted and my mind began to discriminate.

The room was self-luminescent. I could see around me, but there was no light source. It was as if everything gave off its own light; me, the table, the room around me, the very air I felt, for the first time in my life, as a fish must feel water, unaware of it but inseparable from it.

My hearing, too, became acute, and what I heard at first was nothing. No buzz, no hum, no ambient sound. The ship (I did recall it being a ship when we saw it from the road) did not run on anything a man understood, nothing that made noise as even the most sophisticated motor would. I strained to hear something, *anything*, but heard only stillness. Then, slowly, the beating of my heart and the in-out of my breath.

I knew, too, I was not the only one listening.

I became aware of them first as a sensation. A tingling, the very lightest brushing on my skin as if fog had enveloped me—the way humidity feels, there but not there. I looked around, up, to the sides, and saw only the smooth gray that surrounded me. No doors, no windows, no theater from which curious beings could watch as one of them dissected me. Indeed, I couldn't tell if there was one or many. It seemed they were watching me with one gaze, as if, had I been able to return the stare of one, I would be returning the stare of many, and I might well lose my mind from the confusion of such a thing.

Then . . . the sound of something approaching. Not footsteps, not the movement of something that moved on two feet or four, but a *slithering*, that wet sliding sound a snake makes as it hurries toward you across a bare floor. The next thing I knew it was over me, peering down. So close. So foreign and so beautiful, that when I opened my mouth to scream, all that came out was a sigh of awe.

My father used to lock me in the dark as punishment. It was cruel, deliberately taking advantage of my fear—not so much of the dark, but of being unable to see what was across the room, allowing me to imagine the worst. I was, what, three years old? Five? Young enough to know very well there were monsters under the bed and wicked men who came to harm children blinded by the absence of light.

My infractions were minor. Maybe I'd told a small lie, or maybe I'd wandered away from my mother in the grocery store, giving her a fright for which I paid with a greater one. And as terrible as the consequences were, waiting for them was as bad, knowing he would finish out his work day while I sat in a chair he kept just for this. Waiting for him to come home and lay down the law. He never lectured me, never discussed my crimes or how I had crossed the line. He would just say something like, "I told you not to do that," and then he would take me back to the room my mother used for sewing, a strange little triangular room at the northeast corner of the second floor, where the roof sloped sharply down and there was no window. He would shove me in there, turn out the light and lock the door as he shut it behind him.

I did not scream or cry. My father hated weakness as much as he hated disobedience. I always suspected, too, that he would enjoy my distress if I let it out in shouts and pleas, that he would only smile at the sound of my fear and never, ever, come to my rescue.

So many things I imagined in that little back room. Death at the hands of a devil come to suck the breath from my lips, or clawed by rats until my skin hung from my bones and blood soaked the floor. It was, perversely, my only relief: imagining my father's shock at finding me flayed and dead, his regret, his arrest, his conviction and incarceration as the Worst Parent This Town Has Ever Seen.

I did not die. There was no devil but the one who called me son. No rats, no sweet revenge with accompanying headlines. Only me, coming out sometime later, freed by an ultimate captor until the next time.

I was never asked what I'd seen in there—not by my father, not by my mother, not by my older sister who had never been locked in the dark and who found the whole thing amusing. Had I been asked, I would have told them *this* is what I saw, and *that* is what I felt, and someday the opportunity will come for me to go away, up into the sky where I can look down on it all with cool detachment. *Somebody* will want me, will take pains with me, will find me the most curious thing it has ever seen—and if that somebody is from another planet, how much sweeter it will be. For all I knew, they would be coming back for me, having left me by accident with a family I did not belong in. And my alien mother and my alien father will be there, so sorry for misplacing me in the shuffle of their busy alien lives, eager to teach me things any alien child from their planet already knows. There will be a lot of catching up to do. I will be so busy learning my new language and having my new thoughts, that the sorrow of my human family will mean nothing to me. That is what I would have told my family I had seen in the tiny room with the vast darkness, if any of them had asked.

The sensation of floating is a foreign one, the body as unprepared for it as the mind. Human beings do not float, except for that brief time at our beginnings. We may stumble, we may fall, we may find ourselves from time to time suspended between one instant and the next, but *floating* is a luxury for other creatures. Yet that is what I did up there in that corner-less room, floating for the longest time, so long the sun made its way to the horizon, so long the car engine cooled and the seats lost the shapes of our bodies and when I came to, back in the car, the only thing obvious was that we had gone somewhere, but where, and how we got there and back, was knowledge denied us. Not even misted in memory, no vague recollection, but a hole in time, a black hole into which hours and everything that had happened during them had been sucked and obliterated.

I don't know what was done to me. I tried to remember, the way you search for images of what you'd done a drunken night before. But even flashes of color and sound were unavailable to me. *I could see nothing*, struggling to believe there was something there, hoping to capture the face of an alien standing over me as it wrote things down about me. All was blank and dull and silent.

I came to in the back seat, shouting, "Stop the car! Stop the car!"

Charlie had lost his enthusiasm, leaning against the door with his head pressed to the window.

Debs reached up and turned the engine over, shifting into drive and pulling us back onto the road.

And just that quickly we were driving away from it. The clock on the dashboard showed three hours had passed. The last I recalled the engine had died, and now we were speeding away, almost from the same spot we'd been in when Charlie and I first saw that amazing thing out there.

Out there. I turned my head and stared up into an empty sky, a void whose substance was only revealed by a million stars.

"Charlie," I said.

"Shut up," he said. "Shut up, shut up, shut up."

"It's been three hours."

"The bitch sold us crap. My stomach's upset."

"It wasn't the speed, Charlie."

"I'm never doing this again," Debs said. It was the first time she'd spoken since we'd left the highway. "You're going to end up in jail, you're wasting your lives. I'm out of this. God, just get me home."

Just get me home, I thought. That's all I had wanted. Even as a boy locked in the dark. *Just get me home, just get me home.*

I was as alien as they were. Maybe that was the message, the meaning of the whole thing.

Off we drove, back to Bloomington, as if nothing had happened. As if I had not been taken into that thing—sure that Charlie and Debs had been, too. Unless they'd been left sleeping in the car. Aliens can do that, put people to sleep. They can erase our memories, examine us closely and intimately and leave us with no evidence but a persistent suspicion and a feeling we've been raped.

But they can't change time, isn't that curious? They've not mastered that yet. They can't make the sun retreat three hours back into the darkness.

There was nothing in the next morning's paper about strange lights over the farms. No hint of military action in the area. It was as if nothing at all had happened, but I knew it had. I've known it all these years, and every time I drive down a road at night, out there beyond the city, where cars are few and stars are many, I stare out the window looking for a reason to stop the car.

Mark McNease has had six plays produced, the last at New Jersey Repertory Company. His short stories and articles have appeared in numerous publications over 30 years. He spent three years as the Story Editor for foreign co-productions of Sesame Street. *He subsequently won an Emmy for Outstanding Children's Program for* Into the Outdoors, *a children's program he co-created, wrote and produced. He recently finished the 4th book in the* Kyle Callahan Mysteries *series, a gay mystery series featuring an older male couple. He lives in New York City with his husband, Frank Murray. They have a second home in rural New Jersey.* Stop the Car *is a true story ... in parts.*

ABOUT THE EDITORS

Mark McNease, Co-Editor
Mark McNease is an author, publisher and editor. Since 2011 he has published **lgbtSr.org**, a website "where age is embraced and life is celebrated," serving the over-50 LGBTQ community and our friends and allies. His stories and articles have appeared in numerous publications over the past 30 years, beginning with a Los Angeles gay newspaper in the 1980s. He has had six plays produced, the last at New Jersey Repertory Co. He spent 3 years as the Story Editor for foreign co-productions of *Sesame Street*, and subsequently won an Emmy for Outstanding Children's Program for *Into the Outdoors*, a program for 9-to-12-year-olds he co-created, wrote and produced. He recently finished his 4th Kyle Callahan Mystery, a gay mystery series featuring an older male couple. He lives in NYC with his husband, Frank Murray. They have a second home in rural New Jersey.

Stephen Dolainski, Co-Editor
Stephen Dolainski is the founder of **RainbowGray.com**, which celebrates and fosters the unique experiences, wisdom, creativity and

diversity of the LGBT population 50 and older. He has more than 25 years' experience as a writer, editor and educator. He is the author of *Grammar Traps: A Handbook of the 25 Most Common Grammar Mistakes and How to Avoid Them,* which is used in schools and libraries nationwide, and *Romantic Days and Nights in Los Angeles,* a collection of romantically-themed itineraries in and around Los Angeles, and is the co-author of *Words to Learn By: Academic Vocabulary,* a three-book series designed for struggling readers. He has contributed to numerous travel guidebooks, magazines, specialty publications and websites covering travel, lifestyle, business, education and entertainment. He lives in Los Angeles.

CPSIA information can be obtained at www.ICGtesting.com
Printed in the USA
LVOW01s0412280415

436269LV00037B/2252/P